More Million Dollar Mates books

Million Dollar Mates

And, coming soon . . .

Catwalk Queen

Other series by Cathy Hopkins

Mates, Dates

Truth, Dare, Kiss or Promise

Cinnamon Girl

Zodiac Girls

Paparazzi Princess

SIMON AND SCHUSTER

First published in Great Britain in 2011 by Simon and Schuster UK Ltd
A CBS COMPANY

Simon & Schuster UK Ltd
1st Floor
222 Gray's Inn Road
London WC1X 8HB

Typeset by M Rules
Printed and bound in Great Britain.

www.simonandschuster.co.uk
www.cathyhopkins.com

1
Paparazzi

'Are they *always* there, Jess?' asked Meg as we approached Number 1, Porchester Park and saw a bunch of paparazzi gathered outside.

I was walking home from school with my friends, Pia, Meg and Flo. Pretty normal. Apart from the fact that home was *the* flashiest apartment block in town.

'Not always,' I replied. 'It's usually when they've got wind of a celebrity moving in or an A-lister guest visiting one of the residents. Last week, Will Smith was in town and he came to see Alisha's dad.'

To my left, I noticed that Pia had whipped her make-up bag out of her rucksack and was busy applying brick-coloured lippie. Next to her, Flo had shaken her long blonde hair out of its ponytail. Both of them were probably hoping they'd get their photos taken. *No chance*, I thought as they struck a model-like pose – hand on hip, bottom out.

A moment later, when Pia saw that no-one was taking any notice, she crossed her eyes and stuck her tongue out. I knew she was wasting her time trying to get their attention. I wasn't even going to bother untying my hair, although it did look better loose around my shoulders. The paparazzi know who's somebody and who's nobody and four teenagers like Pia, Meg, Flo and me, in our black-and-white school uniforms and coats buttoned up against the bitter December wind, weren't going to cut it, no matter *what* pose Flo struck or daft face Pia pulled.

'*Will Smith?*' said Flo. 'Cool. Did you or Pia see him?'

Pia ran her fingers through her short dark hair to give it more height on top then checked the gathered journalists and photographers again to see if any of them had noticed her yet. They hadn't.

'No,' she said. 'We were at school. Hey, Jess, I reckon we should get in with the paparazzi and ask them to tip us off when they hear that someone fab is on their way.'

'Yeah, right, like *that's* going to happen,' I said. 'Anyway, you know we're not meant to talk to them. Come on, let's get inside. It's freezing out here.'

Pia and I live at Porchester Park. Not in the posh bit where the rich people live, but in the staff area, which is to the side. My dad's the general manager and Pia's mum runs the spa. Both jobs come with a house, though they're nothing fancy, just a bunch of new builds in a mews.

Flo gazed up at the tall apartment block and sighed. 'You guys are so lucky to live here,' she said, with a dreamy look in her big grey eyes. 'The poshest, most amazing address in London with the most glamorous people in the world in and out the door every single day.'

Number 1, Porchester Park doesn't look much from the outside: a tall heap of concrete and glass with an elegant forecourt – pretty much like any five star hotel or apartment block in the city. However, I've seen inside some of the apartments and know what treasures are hidden there: paintings worth millions, rare artefacts from all over the world, lavish marble interiors, gorgeous antiques from foreign palaces, designer kitchens that open out onto vast terraces, bathrooms as big as the whole ground floor of my house, enormous dressing rooms, even a security system designed by the SAS.

Most of the apartments have breathtaking views over London and, on the top floors, it feels like you're up in the clouds. Some of the apartments are awesome, others I think are crass – like bling city – even so, all of them cost loads of money – one resident even has a room used exclusively for their staff to wrap presents! Another has a copy of one of the paintings from the Sistine Chapel in the Vatican on their ceiling. Dad has told me that the cheapest apartment went for twenty mill and the penthouses at the top as much as ninety.

Flo was right. It *was* the poshest address in London, no doubt about it, with residents made up of international celebrities, royalty, wealthy businessmen, their families and personal staff.

'It's not how you'd imagine,' I said, 'not for Pia and me anyway. It's like living just on the edge of wonderland, isn't it, P? We know that this incredible world exists a short distance away but you have to have a magic password to get in.'

'That magic password being ker-*ching:* millions and

trillions,' Pia added. 'Our ten quid pocket money isn't quite in the same league.'

'Understatement,' I said.

'It sounds like Narnia,' said Flo. 'Remember those books where the characters fall through the back of a wardrobe into a magic land?'

I laughed. 'Yeah but the people living in the wonderland here are real, not fairies.' It was typical of Flo to have thought of the Narnia books. She loved fantasy and romanticised any situation.

I had mixed feelings about the place. I'd been living at Porchester Park for a few months now and Pia had moved in a few weeks ago. My first weeks here were well mis. I'd had such great expectations of how it was going to be: how I'd be rocketed into a new life and be moving and grooving with the rich and famous. Ha ha. I'd soon found out that it wasn't like that. It was one set of rules for them and another for us, all dictated by the American director, Mr Knight. For instance: staff and family members can't use the spa, can't talk to the paparazzi, can't use the front entrance, can't keep pets. For the first time in my life, I'd felt inferior, poor and out of place. It was weird. Stuff I'd never felt before. Confused.com, that was me. I'd wanted to leave after a few weeks and go back to my gran's, which was safe and familiar, especially when I was told that I couldn't keep my cat, Dave. That was the last straw. Luckily things changed. The lady running the spa quit and Pia's mum was offered the job and the house that went with it. Hey presto, my best mate in the world was there with me. And I did a deal with a Japanese family in one of the apartments which made it possible to keep Dave. They wanted me to look after their cats when they were away – so, in return, I'd asked that they adopt Dave on paper to keep Um Big Boss Mr Knight happy, so he wouldn't know Dave was a staff pet but he could still live with me. It felt like someone had waved a magic wand. Suddenly I didn't feel so alone. Life at Porchester Park seemed do-able.

'*Why* can't you talk to them?' asked Meg. I noticed that she hadn't bothered to glam up for the photographers. Her attitude is – take me as I am. Lucky for her, she can get away with it. She's pretty, with a heart-shaped face and layered shoulder-length blonde hair which looks highlighted even though it isn't. She looks good whatever she wears, even though she's a tomboy at heart and not into fashion and girlie stuff like the rest of us.

'Dad said I mustn't. *We* mustn't. None of the staff or their relatives can gab about what goes on. The residents want, *insist on*, privacy. They'd hate it if anyone let something slip about their lives.'

'Sometimes the paparazzi offer loads of money,' said Pia, 'just to hear about what celebs eat for breakfast or what colour their bathroom is or even what's in their rubbish. Henry told me he'd heard that one journalist regularly went through celebrities' bins looking for details of their lifestyle.'

'Ew, gross,' said Flo.

Henry lives at Porchester Park too and has recently become Pia's boyfriend, as in proper with regular dates and hanging out at each other's houses. His dad looks after the fleet of fab cars in the underground car park and they also live in one of the staff houses. He and Pia made a cute couple. Henry's dark and stocky with a square handsome face. Pia's got dark hair too, but she's small and pretty with a wide mouth that always seems to be smiling. They look good together, plus both of them are cheeky with a mad sense of humour.

It was still early days for them, though, as it was for me with the two boys I liked. Number one being JJ, who is Jefferson Lewis's son, and number two, Tom, who is in the sixth form at my school. Tom and I had had a couple of kisses and he always flirted when he saw me so maybe it was time to take it further. Or was it? I liked JJ too. We'd only hung out a few times, no kisses yet but I sensed that he liked me. Two boys, both Hunky McDunky, and they were adding to my confused state of mind. Questions whirled around in my head. Which one? Were either of them even interested? How to read the signs they put out? Were they even signs they liked me – or just part of their natural charm? I didn't know. I'd realised recently that I was rubbish at reading boys. They were an alien species with a language all of their own. I certainly wasn't an expert, which is why I had come up with an ingenious plan to wise up. I was going to put it to the girls later and see what they thought . . .

At the front of Porchester Park, I noticed that the doorman, Yoram, had clocked us. He's Israeli, an ex-soldier and not to be messed with. He's not very friendly, unlike his counterpart, Didier, who works the other shifts and is a lovely, handsome French man. Didier is ex-army too but he's *charmant* and treats me like I'm a person, not a speck of dirt to be brushed away. Yoram caught my eye, glanced over at the paparazzi, then back at me. He jerked his thumb in the direction of the staff entrance round the side then brushed an imaginary speck off his immaculate black suit. I felt he was saying that I was that speck, out of place. I got the message. Don't hang around here, move on or else. Four girls looking like they'd just escaped from St Trinian's probably didn't give the right image for the front of the apartment block, where the usual people who came and went were dressed in Chanel, Armani, Prada or some other knobby designer, and were getting in and out of limos with blacked-out windows, rarely arriving on foot.

'We'd better go inside,' I said, 'or He Who Must Be Obeyed will have us shot at dawn.'

Pia glanced over at Yoram. She gave him a cheeky grin and a thumbs-up. 'All right, Yo man?' she called. He glared back at her. 'I'll take that as a yes, then.'

She knew not to push it and linked arms with Flo and Meg, and together we trooped around to the side entrance. I took one last glance at the paparazzi. I felt sorry for them some days as they could be there for hours and on a day like this, they must be well freezing. Some of them knew my name but most days, they ignored me. Today, however, one of them, a short dark-haired woman with a square face, waved. Her name was Bridget O'Reilly. She'd tried to be all pally one evening last week when I was coming back from school. I didn't buy it. Dad had warned me that some of them might try and act like my friend in order to get secrets out of me about Porchester Park. I'd decided that I'd say hi if any of them spoke to me but I wouldn't give anything away.

As I waved back to Bridget, I noticed that there was someone at the back I hadn't seen before. A young handsome man with dark hair was standing slightly apart from the rest of the group and when he saw me looking at him, he pulled up the collar on his mac and turned away.

'Hey Pia,' I said. 'Have you seen that guy over there?'

By the time she turned to look, he'd disappeared.

'Who? Where?' she asked as she looked around.

'Oh, just a journalist I haven't seen before. Cuter than the rest,' I replied.

Hmm, curious, I thought as we reached the side gate. *He hardly looks old enough to be a journalist – maybe he's a student on work experience or maybe . . . a stalker or kidnapper! But if so, who's he after?*

2
The plan

Once inside our house, I lifted Dave off the sofa where he'd been busy cleaning his black-and-white fur. I put out some food for him then filled a pan with milk and began to make hot chocolate. The room soon filled with the soft, sweet smell of cocoa.

Meg and Flo settled on stools at the breakfast bar and Pia draped herself on the sofa that Dave had vacated.

'I wish our house was open plan like yours, Jess,' said Meg. 'It's cool to have one big room where you can watch telly but then get a drink without going far.'

'Has its down sides,' I said. 'I can't get away from Dad and Charlie without going up to my room. And if I want a snack or a drink, they always ask me to make them one too, like I'm their personal slave. Plus Chaz makes rude comments if he sees me eating naughty stuff which is a cheek seeing as he eats rubbish non stop. It's so not fair because he never gets fat.'

'Neither do you,' said Flo. 'You're a skinny minny.'

'No, I'm not. I am so fat,' I said and I made my stomach blow out so that I looked pregnant, which made them all fall about laughing.

'Hey, what are those marks on the wall?' asked Meg as she looked at two pencil dots to the left of the breakfast bar.

'Our height. Charlie and I measure how tall we are,' I said. 'Mum used to do it regularly so she could see how fast we were growing and we decided to carry on the tradition. I was five foot nine and an eighth last time I did it.'

Meg hopped down from her stool. 'Let's do us too,' she said. 'Would your dad mind?'

'Course not,' I said and I got a pencil out of the drawer and put it on the counter.

While I finished making our drinks, Flo marked

everyone on the chart. She was tallest at five foot nine and a quarter, I was next and then Pia at five foot three and Meg at five foot two and a half.

'Cool,' said Meg as she noted her height. 'I'll do it every time I come here so I can see if I'm growing at all or am cursed to be a munchkin my whole life.'

Pia got up and began to do a sideways walk like a crab and sang the munchkin song from *The Wizard of Oz* in a strange voice as if she was being throttled. 'Follow the yellow brick road, follow the yellow brick road, follow, follow, follow, follow, follow the yellow brick road . . .' which made us all fall about laughing again.

Meg's height was her hang up. She hated being titchy because she thought people might not take her seriously. She did martial arts in her spare time to make certain that didn't happen.

Flo took her place back at the bar. 'So, Jess. What's this brilliant plan you wanted to tell us about?'

'I'll tell you in a mo. I promised we'd wait for Alisha to come down. I texted her that we'd be here about four so she should be on her way.'

'We should put her on the height chart too,' Flo suggested. 'She's probably about the same height as me, though, I reckon.'

Alisha is the daughter of Hollywood African-American actor and A-lister, Jefferson Lewis. She lives upstairs in one of the penthouse apartments. After a bumpy start, we'd become mates and I'd promised to let her know when the gang was over next. She is home-schooled and sorely misses her friends back in the States so is really chuffed that we get on now and she has my crowd to hang out with as well as me.

The doorbell rang and Meg went to answer it. Alisha was here, bang on time. 'Hey,' she said, as she came over to the bar and dropped a pink box with a ribbon on the counter. 'Choc chip cookies from Harrods. Major yum alert.'

'Thanks, Alisha,' I said and unwrapped the cookies and put them out on a plate for everyone. She brings something every time she comes – always in the same pretty bags or boxes, always tasting divine and probably costing more than a month of my pocket money. I feel bad sometimes because I can't reciprocate – well, not unless I rob a bank. Instead I make her music CDs with our favourite tracks on so that I don't seem like a taker but sometimes it's hard having a pal in a pocket money bracket that's way out of your league. As always, she looked immaculate in designer jeans that fitted perfectly and a blue silk top. I also noticed that she was carrying a camera.

'Taking pics?' I asked.

'I'd like to take one of you guys,' she said, 'to send to my friends back home so that they don't think I've moved to Planet Loser and have no-one to play with.'

'But we've got our school uniforms on,' Flo objected. 'We look rubbish.'

Alisha rolled her eyes. 'Would you like me to send for my stylist before we do the shots?'

'Yes!' chorused Pia and Flo.

'*Joking*,' said Alisha, although we all knew that the Lewis family had someone on call to come and tart them up anytime they wanted. Alisha had her long curly hair blow-dried regularly and her nails were always immaculately polished in dark purple. 'You guys look great. Just smile. As the saying goes, of all the things you wear, your expression is the most important.'

'Ew, vomit,' said Pia. 'Is that like, American New Age speak?'

Alisha laughed. 'Yeah. And it's true,' she aimed her camera. 'So smile, guys. Think bee-oo-tiful and you will be.'

Meg and Flo ducked down and Pia put her hand over her face.

'No pictures, no pictures,' she said. 'Take one when I have a party outfit on.'

Alisha sighed and put her camera away. 'OK, OK, I'll take one some other time.'

I gave everyone their hot chocolates and Pia and I settled on the sofa and Alisha, Meg and Flo on bean bags.

'Jess has a brilliant plan to tell us, Alisha. So come on, Jess,' said Meg. 'We're all ears.'

'Right,' I said as I took a sip of my drink. 'Boys. That mysterious species that we have to share the planet with.'

'What about them?' asked Meg.

'Exactly. What about them? I've realised that in the world of boys, girls and relationships, I am a dud student. Up until a few years ago, boys were just smelly noisy creatures to be avoided at all costs.'

'Some still are,' said Meg. 'Like Adrian Nelson at school. He smells of old socks.'

'Ah yes but some *aren't* to be avoided. Some have grown up to be handsome Hunky McDunkies who have a strange effect on me and my knees and my head and my stomach. Like you, I spent years pushing boys away in playgrounds, wrestling with them when they pulled my hair and annoyed me but now, well, I want to get to know some of them – know them as in a-hubba-hubba—'

'Snog city here you come, you mean,' said Pia.

'Not just that. I'd like more. I'd like to have a relationship with one. I've never had a proper boyfriend, not like you and Henry—'

'Me neither,' said Meg.

'Nor me,' said Alisha. 'I mean, I've kissed a few boys but never had, like, a soulmate.'

'Nor me,' I said, 'I'd like to be in love as in everlasting and true like Edward and Bella in *Twilight* but I always seem to blow it and say and do the wrong thing. I've realised that I have a lot to learn.'

'I wouldn't worry,' said Pia. 'I don't think we have vampires at our school.'

'You know what I mean, Pia.'

The girls all nodded and Alisha pointed at herself. 'Tell me about it,' she agreed.

'I don't know how I'm supposed to be a girl that they like,' I continued. 'I mean, what *do* they like? I've spent so long avoiding boys because they're a pain but now things have changed, *I've* changed –

but how am I supposed to make the reversal from boy repeller to boy attractor? From the girl who would say, push off you idiot, you stupid git, to one who would say, hello handsome, how about a date? How do you do it and still come across as cool and sophisticated? I just don't know. What does a boy even look for in a girl? Loads of girls in our year have been dating since Year Eight. How have they done it? Do they know something I don't? I was feeling like a real love loser, then I thought, no, I should do something about it. I'm *not* a loser. I won't be. So. Sink or swim. Love or lose. I'm going to learn about boys. Why not? If you don't know about a subject, you go to the library, right? You do some homework, read some books. That's what I propose we do. Study boys. Do some research. I'm going to become a boy expert – the winner of hearts!'

'Yay. Go, Jess,' said Alisha. 'That's the spirit. I love it.'

'You just be yourself,' said Pia, who has always been more confident than me when it comes to boys. 'If you try too hard, like coming out with chat-up lines or whatever from a text book, you'll come across as fake. Boys'll spot that right away.'

'I don't mean to be fake, Pia. I mean to ask around,

ask people we know who've had not just one boyfriend but maybe one or two. *Experienced* girls and boys. We could ask around, then pool our collective knowledge. What do you think? Between us and everyone else we know, we ought to find out *some* stuff worth knowing.'

The girls considered what I'd said.

'I'm in,' said Alisha.

'Me too,' chorused Meg and Flo.

'And me,' said Pia. 'But, how exactly?'

'That's what today's meeting is about. How about we work out some questions to ask about all the things we feel ignorant about, which for me, is most things. Then we could post them on facebook for boys *and* girls to answer.'

'Awesome,' said Alisha. 'I'll get JJ to ask his mates too. He might be my brother but he has some cool friends back in the States.'

I shot a look at Pia. I hoped that she wasn't going to blurt out that I fancied JJ. Even though Alisha and I were mates now, I couldn't risk telling her in case she told him. I was also worried that he was out of my league and that because his family was loaded, he would only fancy girls from his world.

We spent the next half hour chomping our way

through Alisha's divine cookies while we worked out our questions.

'Ask the boys what first attracts them to a girl,' Alisha suggested. 'Like, what are they looking for?'

'And what turns them off,' Meg added. 'My brother is always on about how he doesn't like girls who plaster on too much make-up.'

'And Charlie says he doesn't like girls who smoke because it makes their breath smell,' I added.

'Someone's coming,' said Pia as we heard a noise at the front door. Moments later, my brother appeared. He glanced over us as he took off his coat. Flo went pink, as always. She loves him big time although nothing has ever happened between them. Shame really, because they'd look good together. They both have a look about them that's old-fashioned, but not in a naff way. Charlie looks like a handsome poet from the Victorian era with his long floppy hair and, out of school, Flo always dresses in vintage clothes she's picked up from Portobello market. Both of them are dreamy-eyed romantics – though Charlie more about music than girls.

'What are you lot up to?' he asked. 'You're looking decidedly guilty.'

'Nothing,' I said.

'Not true,' said big-mouth Pia. 'We're doing a love survey.'

'Yeah, Chaz,' called Meg. 'Come and tell us everything there is to know about boys and what they want from girls.'

Flo clearly felt more courageous having heard Meg and Pia. 'Yeah, come and sit next to me and answer Jess's questionnaire,' she said.

Charlie looked worried. It wasn't that he didn't like Flo or the other girls, he just preferred music and playing his guitar.

'Er, just remembered, got something to do, some place to be,' he said. 'Laters.'

Flo's face fell. 'This idea of yours is happening just in time, Jess,' she said as Charlie bolted up the stairs. 'I really do need to know how to be with boys. It's not just you who needs help. So put this question on the list: how do you let a boy know you like him without scaring him off?'

Later that night when they'd all gone, I sat with Dave on my lap and put the list of questions on the computer ready to post on facebook. A ping sound told me that an email had arrived.

It was from Pia. She'd sent a photo of an enormous

buxom woman dressed as Boudicca in a helmet with horns, long plaits and wearing a big brass bra and carrying an axe as if ready to do battle.

Underneath it, she'd written:

> Dear Ms Hall. In response to your on-going research into the mysterious subject of boys, I would like to say that one should always go pulling wearing a similar outfit to the one above. This look has never failed me. I have always got exactly what I want wearing it, be it flirting, chatting up a boy, kissing or breaking up. When they see my axe and helmet, they just *know* I mean business.

I loved having Pia as a mate. She made me laugh daily. I looked back at the intimidating woman. Weapons were one approach but somehow I was hoping that I could win a boy's heart *without* having to beat him into submission.

3
Perfect break?

'So . . . your homework for the Christmas holidays,' said Mrs Moran, our English teacher, with a well fake smile.

A groan spread through the classroom.

'But *Miss*, it's the holidays,' said Chrissie O'Connell.

Mrs Moran laughed. She's OK for a teacher, round and jolly, like a fat golden hen, and she doesn't mind when someone in class talks back to her.

'Exactly,' said Mrs Moran, 'and I hope you all have a very merry time. However, we don't want your brains to get rusty, do we? No, we don't, which is why

I've come up with a project to keep you active. Think of it as an early Christmas present.' The class groaned again. 'The perfect winter holiday,' she continued. 'I want you to think about what that might be and then write about it. You can choose your angle—'

'No school, no homework, *that* would be the perfect holiday,' Tony Davidson called from the back of class.

'Yeah, Miss, it's like asking us to write about what we did over the summer,' said Jason Clery. 'That's, like, so junior school.'

'Come on, class, where's your enthusiasm?' asked Mrs Moran. 'It's not a difficult task. It might even be enjoyable. I'm asking you to think about what the festive season means to different people. To someone on their own, or someone in hospital. Someone homeless. What it means in other cultures, maybe. What would be a really perfect winter holiday? Is it the movie version with log fires inside and snow outside? A family all together? Presents, masses of delicious food and television or perhaps a celebration of the birth of Christ? But then what about people of other faiths? What would the perfect holiday celebration be for a Muslim or Hindu or Buddhist? I think it could be a great project. You have a lot of scope and a lot to think about.'

Although I got what she was saying, my heart sank. My perfect winter holiday would be a Christmas with my mum back. She died of cancer just over a year ago in early December. I could write pages on an *imperfect* Christmas because that's what it was last year. An awful, miserable time. Charlie and I were at Gran's and although her place is as homely as you can get, even she didn't feel like decorating that year. It wouldn't have been right when the one person who should have been there wasn't. I'd felt numb. Charlie and I just sat in front of the telly and watched one movie after the other, but if you asked me what they were about, I wouldn't know and I don't think he would either. Mum used to make Christmas so special. She really loved it. As soon as she got out the decorations, she'd put on her favourite Christmas CD by Phil Spectre and she'd sing along at the top of her voice. She always made Charlie and me wear Santa hats and well naff jumpers with holly or reindeer on them. It was tradition, *our* family tradition, and she said such things were important in making Christmas memorable. She was right about that.

One year, she dressed up as a Christmas tree. Who could ever forget that? The costume was hysterical, a pointy green hat like the top of a tree, then a tunic dress which you put your arms through and it widened out towards the skirt like the branches of a fir tree.

Mad, but that was Mum. She liked to dress up for any occasion, any excuse. She'd also make her own mince pies and cake and for weeks, our house would smell of nutmeg, cinnamon and oranges. She went the whole hog: advent calendars, red candles that smelt of frankincense and sandalwood, tinsel everywhere, even on the taps in the bathroom!

We always had a great tree, a real one that smelt of pine and was decked with loads of red and gold baubles with silver and gold tinsel circling from top to bottom. She loved the card sending too – no copping out and doing it by email for her. She'd spend ages buying and wrapping presents and never got bored with it like Aunt Maddie did. Aunt M said doing Christmas cards year after year made her feel like she was trapped in a groundhog day. She gave up doing it years ago and donated the money for cards and gifts to charity, telling us that Christmas was nothing but a commercial venture.

One year, she gave my and Charlie's Christmas present money to a farm in Africa. Typical of her as Missgoodietwoshoes-savetheworld but so different to Mum's attitude which was Christmas was a time to celebrate life, loved ones, a time to be joyful and blow the expense.

Mum bought the cards, gifts and all the seasonal trimmings *and* donated to charity. That was her attitude to everything – yes, put something back into the world but make sure you have a good time while you're here too.

An image of Mum in the kitchen wearing her red-and-white Santa hat and singing, 'It's getting to feel a lot like Christmas,' flashed through my head and my eyes filled with tears. I missed her as much now as when she first went – more even, because the longer it was since she died, the more final it seemed. She hadn't gone away for a break, on a holiday. No. Wherever she'd gone, she wasn't coming back. Not even for Christmas. It sucked.

Pia turned around in her seat and gave me a sympathetic look. She sensed what I was feeling and she was right. *I say bah humbug to your project*, Mrs *Moran*.

*

'Have you decided what you're going to do at Christmas?' asked Pia as we filed out of class in the break.

I shrugged. 'Not sure. Ignore it? Hide under a holly bush and only come out when it's all over.'

Pia linked arms with me. 'I know it's hard for you but I remember your mum and how she loved it all. It was her favourite time. She'd hate to see you unhappy. I reckon you should carry on the traditions she started, get into it all big time like she did. Do it for her.'

'I . . .' I had no defence. Pia was right, and Mum had said almost exactly the same words to me in her last week. She said she was sorry she couldn't be around and that I was to try my best to be brave and to celebrate the joy of being alive and the spirit of Christmas. I'm sure that she'd have understood that I couldn't do it for her last year but maybe this year, I could. I *should*.

'It's our first Christmas at Porchester Park,' Pia continued, 'Mum told me that the decorators are coming in this week to do a number in reception. I bet they'll make it look fabulous, plus we'll be together. Maybe we should throw a party. Get Tom and the others from school to come. We could put up a ton of mistletoe for snog sessions.'

The idea of seeing Tom over the holidays did appeal. Maybe we could take things to the next level, from flirting and the occasional kiss to being an item. My first proper boyfriend.

'OK, yeah. I guess we could have a cool yule with no school,' I said.

'You're a poet and you didn't know it,' Pia added.

I went into my version of what was meant to be street dancing but had a feeling looked more like I'd put my hand in an electric socket and was having a seizure.

'Cool yule, outta school,' I said in a rap style.

Pia joined in. 'Don't be a fool, no rules.'

I grabbed my crotch à la the late Michael Jackson and attempted to moonwalk backwards. Of course that was the moment Tom came round a corner. When he saw me and Pia, he rolled his eyes and grinned. 'Ah, the crazy twins. You 'ave ze ants in ze pants, ah oui?'

'Mais non, dude, we're getting down,' I said. I did a knee drop then jerky spin in what was meant to be a cool smooth move but sadly, lost my balance and toppled into the wall.

'Keep taking the medication, Hall,' said Tom. 'You clearly aren't well.'

'You just don't recognise talent when you see it,' said Pia.

Tom laughed then looked right into my eyes, 'Oh yes I do,' he said in a suggestive voice. I blushed and inside, I felt my stomach rise as if a soft breeze had lifted it then it floated back down, making me feel disorientated. Tom always has this effect on me. I love him being flirty in public, though, and noticed a couple of passing girls check us out. He's one of the cutest boys in our school, tall and handsome with light brown shoulder-length hair, flawless skin and eyes the most astonishing jade green. Trouble is, he knows he has babe appeal and that half the school fancies him.

Art was my next class and I spent the whole lesson fantasising about what Tom and I could do together over the next few weeks. Winter scenes from every slushy movie I'd ever seen played through my head: we could roast marshmallows by the fire then snuggle up on the sofa to watch old black-and-white movies, maybe go ice skating up on Hampstead Heath then to a cosy café for hot chocolates. I could see it all so clearly – him laughing in the snow at something I'd said, a look of delight on his face when he unwrapped some perfect present I'd found him.

Oh yes, the next few weeks could be romance heaven for a new couple like us. I was beginning to change my mind about the whole holiday, in fact – a lovely time with Tom, then Christmas Day with Gran. Fab. Gran did a great turkey dinner with all the trimmings and her house was big and comfy. I felt safe there and there were always people dropping in. Maybe this year, it could be ding dong merrily on high and a time to deck the halls with Christmas holly. Yes, I decided, it was the season to be jolly and I would be!

'Let's go and look for Tom again,' Pia suggested in the lunch break. Now that she had a proper boyfriend, she was as eager as I was that I had one too. 'He'll probably be in the dining room. Let's go and see if we can find him.'

We made our way through the maze of school corridors and up to the first floor. Our luck was in because Tom was mooching about outside the canteen with his mates Josh Tyler and Roy Mason.

'Ah. Your personal love slave has arrived,' said Josh Tyler when he saw me. 'Hey, Hall, Tom was just saying that he'd like you to get your clothes off and wait for him in the gym.'

Tom rolled his eyes. 'You know I didn't say that, Jess.'

'Yeah right,' I said. 'And anyway, like I would strip in this weather for anyone. Don't you know it's two degrees outside today?'

'Sorry about my crass friend,' said Tom and he came towards me, put his arm around my waist and pulled me close to him. 'But if it really is two degrees outside then all the more reason for me to warm you up.'

Behind him, Pia mouthed that she'd see me later then disappeared back down the stairs. She understands about giving a couple space, unlike Roy and Josh who were hanging around watching the whole scene. I decided to ignore them. Tom had his arms around me, that was what was important. I snuggled into him and it seemed like the perfect time to ask him about hanging out in the holidays. 'Er, Tom . . . now that we're . . . er . . .'

'We're what?' asked Tom with a quizzical look and a quick glance at his mates. *Back-track, back-track*, I told myself. *Maybe it's too early to refer to us as 'we'. Boys don't like being pinned down.*

'We . . . I mean me,' I continued. 'I was wondering if you wanted to get together over the holidays and you know . . .'

I heard Josh snigger and Tom let me go and stood back a step. 'Get together?'

'Yes. Maybe—'

Tom shrugged. 'Um . . . not sure what I'm doing yet, Jess. I . . . I don't really do plans. I prefer to stay loose, not be tied down to anything. Know what I'm saying?'

I felt a thud of disappointment in the pit of my stomach. This wasn't going well and my earlier fantasies faded like a snowball in an oven. I got what he was saying all right.

'Er . . . yeah, course. Keep it loose. Me too.' I stepped away and went towards the stairs.

'Hey, you OK? You look kind of upset,' Tom called after me. Josh and Roy were still looking on as though they were enjoying my discomfort. I cursed myself for asking Tom about hanging out while they were there.

'Me, nah. Never. Loose as a goose, that's me.' Inside I felt like dying. What was I saying? Loose as a goose? What idiot says mad things like that? Me. That's who. I don't even know what it means. I am such a love loser.

'Cool,' said Tom. 'And I'm sure I'll be over to see Charlie at some point, practise some sounds with him and that. Maybe catch you then.'

'Yeah. Right.'

No lingering looks or suggestive comments this time, I noticed. *They say girls are changeable but I really don't get boys*, I thought as I thumped down the stairs.

My whole mood felt deflated as I went into the girls' cloakroom and into a cubicle. As I put the seat down and got my phone out to text Pia to come and meet me, I heard the door open and close and someone come in.

'There's going to be a few good parties,' said a girl's voice. 'Tom Robertson said he'll probably have one at some point. Yay.'

I froze mid text.

'He is *so* cool. I think you're in with a chance there,' said another voice.

Ohmigod! I knew those voices. Ros Gambier and Peta Howarth from Year Eleven. Only two of the best-looking, most sophisticated girls in the school. One dark, the other blonde, they both have style and a band of wannabes copy their every move, haircut or nail colour.

So it *wasn't* that Tom didn't want to make plans. He just didn't want to make them with me!

Tom Robertson, I hate you, I thought as I heard the

door open and close again as the girls left. I felt such a fool. I should have known. What would he want with a great stupid buffoon like me? I didn't know how to be with a boy, not really, and I couldn't be sophisticated if I tried. I always ended up doing or saying something daft but then boys don't always want girls to be funny. They don't want anyone moving in on them too much, either. You have to be cool but not too cool. You have to show you like them but not too much or they run off like scared deer. *I hate boys. They do my head in*, I decided. *I thought Tom was into me and we had something special going on. What an idiot I am. I started feeling all this lovely slushy stuff I've never felt before then he does the cool I-don't-care act like I mean nothing to him. It hurts. I wish he was my boyfriend and not available to the whole school. No, I don't. I hate him and wouldn't go out with him if he begged me. Most of all, I hate the dull ache I feel in the pit of my stomach. Love sucks.*

My phone bleeped that I had a text from Pia.

Where R U?

In doldrums. Loo. Ground floor, I texted back.

Minutes later, I heard Pia's foosteps.

'You in there?'

'Yep and I'm not coming out. I am going to stay

here like that Moaning Myrtle ghost in *Harry Potter*, the one who lives in the toilet.'

'Could get very smelly and boring.'

'Don't care.'

'What's happened? Last time I saw you, you were cuddling up to lover boy.'

Through the closed door, I told her the latest.

'So?' she said when I'd finished. 'Stuff him. There are other boys. JJ Lewis, for instance. Imagine how Tom would feel if you got off with *him*. And there's still your gran's at Christmas to look forward to. Don't let a stupid boy bring you down. If he can't see that he'd be lucky to have you as his girlfriend, then he's not worth it. Come on, Jess, come out.'

I opened the loo door.

'Least you have options,' said Pia. 'Another day, another boy. Not all girls have two boys they like.'

'They probably do. The important thing is, does the boy like you back? In my case, no.' I replied. 'There's clearly something wrong with me and I repel boys.' My confidence had taken a knock and if Tom wasn't that into me, maybe JJ wouldn't be either. 'Unrequited love sucks, Pia.'

She made the L for loser sign with her thumb and

index finger on her forehead. 'What? Planet loser, population you? No way. You're a great-looking girl, Jess Hall. I don't buy this loser talk. When the going gets tough, the tough move on. A new day, a new boy.'

'Nah. I'm off boys forever,' I said. 'I ca-an't tay-ake the pai-ain-n-n.'

Pia burst out laughing. 'You're such a drama queen.'

'It's OK for you. You're going to hang out with Henry after school while I'm going back to the gloom of my lonely room where I'll sit in the dark and listen to tragic love songs.'

Pia laughed even more. So much for getting any sympathy from her.

When I got home, I went to my facebook discussion page.

Extraordinary revelations about boys by Jess Hall, I wrote.

1) Don't ever assume that you know what is going on in a boy's head. You probably don't.

2) Boys do your head in.

As I was typing, an email came through from Pia.

It said:

> Jess, add this to your research. Henry just told me to tell you this. Boys act differently when they're with their mates, as if they have to prove that they're cool and indifferent. They'll never be slushy or lovey dovey if they have mates watching them, even if they're nuts about you. If you like a boy, get him on his own. Don't go out in big groups and try to stake your claim on him when his friends are around – or at least not until he's hooked. Geddit? Tom was into you when he was by himself and only acting Mr Cool because Josh and Roy were watching.

I read the email a few times. *Maybe*, I thought. *But even if it's true and Tom was just being non-committal because his mates were there, it still doesn't change the situation. Pia's loved up at her house with Henry and I am still here on my own, sans boyfriend.*

4
Christmas wishes

'Hey, Jess, got a moment?' called a female voice from the crowd of journalists. I turned to look and saw that the small, dark-haired lady, Bridget, was coming over to me through the sleet and rain. She looked like she was in her forties, had a soft Irish accent and as she approached, she gave me a big smile, but then they all act like I am their friend on the occasions that they speak to me.

'I . . . I've got to go in,' I said. I didn't want to be seen talking to her in case I got in trouble with Yoram, who was watching me like a hawk from the front door.

'Ah, I'm not going to bite,' she said as she stood beside me and looked in the direction of Porchester Park. 'I see they're putting the decorations up in reception. It's going to look just lovely, so it is.'

I nodded. It was already looked opulent inside the apartment block. Winter Wonderland was the theme – all very tasteful and extravagant with a four-metre tree in the corner of reception decked in silver baubles and big white ribbons.

'I suppose some people will be coming back for Christmas, won't they?' Bridget continued with a shiver against the cold wind. 'Maybe some your own age from their schools?'

I glanced over at Yoram, who made the tiniest movement to the left with his chin. I knew what that meant. Get inside. 'I don't know,' I said, 'but I really do have to go now. I'm freezing.'

'Me too. Yes, go on,' said Bridget. 'Go in and get yourself warmed up. Broken up from school, have you now?'

I nodded. 'Today. Yep. Holidays, hurrah,' I said with more conviction than I felt. I'd been hoping to bump into Tom around school before the end of term and get an invite to his party but the sixth form had broken up earlier than the rest of us. I hadn't seen him since our last awkward meeting when we agreed to 'keep it loose', so the usual joy of the last day at school was tinged with disappointment for me.

I hurried round to the staff entrance and noticed that over to the left of the crowd of paparazzi was a homeless man sitting in the doorway of an empty shop. I'd seen him there a few times lately, wrapped up in an old blanket and cardboard box. I usually crossed the road to avoid him as sometimes he liked to shout – not at me, but at the whole world. Yoram and Didier had moved him on a few times as no way was his presence desirable for the posh Porchester Park image, but he kept coming back. I had to admire him for that. He wanted to be homeless in the posh part of town. Standing up to Yoram took some courage and it made me smile to think that the residents spent millions to live in the most exclusive location in London and yet they couldn't stop an old tramp coming to sit in a doorway and watch the world go by.

Bridget had been right about the residents, there *were* people expected back for the holiday – mainly teenagers who'd been at boarding school abroad. I'd seen the list a few weeks ago but I wasn't going to tell

Bridget who they were or when they were arriving. Dad had drilled it into me – no discussing the comings and goings of anyone who lived here. Some of the newcomers sounded exciting, like a Russian boy my age called Alexei Petrov, though I hadn't seen him around yet. There was also a Saudi prince who'd apparently arrived a few days ago. I hadn't seen him, either, but then I'd hardly seen any of his family apart from the occasional glimpse when they appeared like a flock of black birds from above and disappeared quickly into waiting limos. They lived at the top on the far side of the apartment block and had four apartments: two for the family, two for staff and apparently an apartment close by in another block for even more staff.

The only newcomer I *had* met was a Japanese girl called Riko Mori. I already knew her mum and dad and nine-year-old sister, Sakura, because of our arrangement that I look after their Persian cats when they were away. Riko looks about my age, is slightly built and very pretty. She has amazing style – a mix of preppy and eccentric – like she mixes gingham with tartan and leopard skin and wear sports shoes. Stuff that shouldn't go together but somehow works. She looks original, that's for sure. Some days, she wears her shoulder-length hair in bunches which would make her look young if she didn't wear heavy black eye makeup and bright red lipstick. Other days, she mixes vintage evening clothes with something new and street and puts something mad in her hair like a small toy. She wasn't friendly the first time we met, but not unfriendly either, like she was sizing me up before she decided if I was a person worth knowing or not. Today, when I got to the staff entrance, I was surprised to see her in the courtyard wearing an ankle-length padded coat, an enormous pink scarf and big dark glasses, even though the sky was grey and overcast.

'Hey, Riko. You lost?' I asked.

She shook her head. 'Not exactly.' She speaks perfect English, unlike Sakura who speaks only a little and their mother who speaks none at all. She indicated the gate behind me. 'I'm . . . just finding my way around. Is that another entrance?' she asked as she looked at the gate I'd just come through.

'Yes. It's for staff. There are five houses here so we use the side entrance,' I said. I gestured at the mews houses laid out around the paved courtyard.

Riko followed my gaze. 'I see. But isn't there also a way out the back somewhere?'

I nodded. 'There's a door and a gate at the back of the block behind the service lift.'

'Service lift?'

'Yeah. It's used for deliveries and workmen. The residents' staff use it too.'

'I see. Thank you. It's all so new to me.'

'I know. It took me a while too. It felt like a maze when I first moved in.'

'And the doormen?' Riko continued. 'Are there some at the back and staff entrance as well?'

'No. Just Yoram and Didier at the front. The other gates are always locked if they're not being used.'

'So you have a key?'

I shook my head. 'A code. Don't worry, no-one can get in here.'

'Or out,' she said with a grim expression. 'Thank you, you've been most helpful.' With a glance behind her, she disappeared back into the residents' lobby.

'No prob,' I called after her. 'Just let me know if I can help with anything else.' I wondered if she was feeling trapped. Alisha told me that sometimes she wished she could roam freely like Pia and I did, instead of having to go everywhere with a minder in tow watching her every move.

I hurried inside to collect Charlie. We were due to

go over to Gran's to help decorate her tree. I was really looking forward to it and had been out to get some purple ribbons to make bows for the branches.

Charlie was waiting for me inside, sitting at the breakfast bar eating a bag of crisps.

'You ready?'

'Yumph,' Charlie replied through a mouthful.

'You need a haircut,' I said.

Charlie pulled his tousled hair over his eyes. 'Yes, Sir,' he said. 'But I like it longer. And so do the girls.'

'Oo. Get you, you babe magnet,' I said. Actually Charlie *could* be a babe magnet. He didn't have the teen movie star looks that Tom had but he had an open, friendly face and dark, honey-coloured eyes that were kind. Girls liked him but, unlike Tom, he wasn't aware of it. 'Hey. Shall we put our Christmas jumpers on?'

Charlie opened his jacket to reveal that he was already wearing his – a red cable polo neck with a big reindeer head on the front. Mum had knitted it while she was in hospital.

'Very tacky,' I said.

Charlie grinned.

I raced upstairs to put mine on – a cream one with a Christmas tree on the front. I looked at my reflection in the mirror. *Hmm, a time to look cool and a time to look mad,* I thought as I reached into a drawer to add a pair of holly-shaped earrings. *Mum would have approved.* Although she had worked in the fashion industry when she was alive and had a great eye for putting together a stylish look, she still loved a chance to dress up like a nutter when she could. I didn't mind as long as no-one like Tom or JJ saw me. I'm not sure they'd understand. They'd probably just think I was naff.

Five minutes later, Charlie and I set off to catch the bus to Gran's.

'I'm really looking forward to Christmas now,' I said as we made our way out of the staff entrance.

'Good girl,' said Charlie. 'Me too. As Mum always said, life is what you make of it.'

'I know. Christmas Day at Gran's with all our old family traditions,' I said. 'No one does Christmas dinner like Gran: big turkey, all the trimmings, it's going to be fab. A few movies, chilling on the sofa, bliss. We'll have a good time.'

Charlie nodded. 'For Mum.'

'For Mum,' I agreed.

'You know Dad has to work on the twenty-fifth, don't you, Jess?' asked Charlie.

I nodded. 'But we'll be back home on Boxing Day and can spoil him then.'

As we were waiting at the bus-stop, I saw the Lewises' limo draw up outside the front of Porchester Park. Jefferson Lewis got out and the paparazzi went into a frenzy of taking pictures as he went inside. He looked every inch the A-lister he was and even though he was wearing dark glasses, he exuded charisma, like he had an extra shine on him that the rest of us don't have. JJ got out after him and spotted Charlie and me at the bus stop. He waved, called something to his dad then came over to join us. JJ stood out just like his dad. He is well fit, tall with broad shoulders, handsome with great cheekbones and always impeccably dressed. Today he was wearing a knee-length overcoat that looked like cashmere and a red-and-blue striped scarf. He and Tom are so different. Tom always looks like he's just got out of bed and thrown yesterday's clothes on. JJ always looks neat, his clothes newly laundered and pressed. I quickly buttoned my coat right up so he wouldn't see my jumper.

'Just going to get some gum,' said Charlie as JJ got closer. Typical Charlie. He knew that I had a crush on JJ so was giving me some space to be with him.

I saw the paparazzi watching us but they didn't take any photos. Son of celeb talks to one of the staff was clearly not newsworthy, plus Henry had told me that Mr Lewis had told the paparazzi that he would agree to have his picture taken occasionally in return for them leaving his children alone.

'Hey, Jess,' said JJ. He even smelt expensive, a subtle scent of lime aftershave. 'How's it going?'

'Good. Getting ready for Christmas. You?'

JJ gave me one of his mega watt smiles. 'Yeah,' he leant forward. 'Actually, I'm hoping to spend it with someone special—'

'JJ,' called Jefferson Lewis from the courtyard.

JJ acknowledged his dad and moved back a step. 'Later, hey?' he said. 'Catch you when you come up to see Alisha.'

'Later.' I felt my knees go weak. By the way he'd lowered his voice and leant towards me, I was sure he meant me when he'd said someone special. It had to be me. *Tom Robertson, who needs you?* I thought as I watched JJ make his way back over to Porchester Park.

When we arrived at Gran's, she had hot apple juice with cinnamon and mince pies waiting for us. Yum scrum. As we curled up on the sofa in front of the fire, I thought about how to decorate and whether my purple ribbons would work – the tree at Gran's would be totally different to the one at Porchester Park. Gran had a box of decorations that she'd had for years and rather than there being a theme, it was more like throwing whatever was in the box onto the branches: red, gold, purple, silver, white, loads of tinsel, angels, old wooden trains, chocolate coins, it didn't matter and it still managed to look good.

Each decoration told a story, like the 'angels' that I'd made in junior school in art class – they looked more like worms with wings but Gran had never minded. She liked the sentimentality of them. Various other angels that had been added over the years: a punk one that Charlie had made in art class, a rag doll cherub that Mum had seen in Liberty's and hadn't been able to resist, plus a collection of stars in different sizes and styles.

We didn't choose one for the top of the tree, we usually put them all on. Less is more was never an attitude that Mum believed in at Christmas. I liked both approaches, the posh and elegant at Porchester and the funky chaos at Gran's. My purple ribbons would be just fine on there along with everything else.

'So, where's the tree, Gran?' I asked.

'Ah. Yes. That. I have something to tell you,' said Gran. She looked nervous and Gran was usually Queen of Calm. She didn't look her seventy years of age. She always dressed beautifully in layers of colourful bohemian clothes and devore scarves and her white hair was cut into an immaculate bob. Today, though, even her hair looked dishevelled.

'Has something happened?' I asked. 'Are you all right?'

'Sit down both of you,' she said.

I felt a flutter of anxiety. In the past, the words, 'sit down both of you,' had always come before bad news.

'What is it, Gran?' asked Charlie, who looked as worried as I was.

'Nothing bad,' said Gran. 'Not at all. No. It's just I've . . . I've had an invite, or at least not an invite, someone has dropped out, a bunch from my art class are going, only five days and now there's a place but—'

'What, Gran? Dropped out of what?' I asked.

'Sorry,' said Gran. 'I'm rambling, aren't I? Florence. I'm talking about Florence, in Italy. Remember my friend Lily?'

Charlie and I nodded.

'Well, she was going to Florence on an art trip over Christmas. A bunch of them have booked an apartment in a palazzo. I could show you on the Net, fabulous and the views out of the window, well . . . Anyway, there's to be a workshop at the Uffizi gallery. Life drawing. They'd asked if I wanted to go but I couldn't afford that kind of money. Anyway, Lily's had to drop out. Her husband's not well and she's offered me the place. It's all been paid for and she won't take anything – just doesn't want to see it go to waste. Christmas present, she said. I won't go if you two don't want me to. I said I had to talk to you first.'

'You must go, Gran,' said Charlie immediately. 'Of course you must.'

'Over Christmas?' I asked.

Gran nodded and looked for my reaction. I swallowed, then smiled and nodded. 'Course you must.' I knew how much it would mean to her. Apart from her family, painting is her life. She's good at it too. She does watercolours and some portraiture in pastels. She's had exhibitions. People buy her work. A chance to go and study at the Uffizi would be a dream come true for her.

She came and sat on the sofa between Charlie and me and put her arms around both of us. She smelt of baking and roses. 'Are you sure? I've been agonising about it, I mean it's Christmas and . . .'

She didn't need to say any more. She was asking us to do Christmas without her as well as Mum. I couldn't help it but the idea filled me with dread. Granddad had died a few years ago so Gran hadn't just lost a daughter recently, she'd lost her husband too. I knew I should do anything to make her happy – just like I knew she'd do for me.

My hopes for Christmas were once again disappearing in front of my eyes but I was determined not to let Gran know. If she got the slightest inkling that I was unhappy about the trip, she'd refuse to go.

'Actually, Gran, it's a bit of a relief because Charlie and I felt bad about deserting Dad. He has to work but I think he'd like it if we were there so at least he could pop in on his breaks and be with us some of the time. It's our first Christmas with him and we felt bad about leaving him, didn't we, Chaz? We can make the mews house look amazing. No. I think it's worked out for the best all around.'

Over Gran's shoulder, Charlie winked at me. That was me, good girl, brave girl, only inside, I felt the opposite. I felt raw. Yet again, life wasn't working out how I imagined it should. I'd like to have cuddled up to Gran and her safe, familiar scent and held on to her like a five-year-old but I also knew that I mustn't let her know that. I didn't want to spoil her special trip by acting like a baby.

At least there's some time with JJ to look forward to, I told myself as I felt a dark cloud descending. *I mustn't give in to doom and gloom*. Mum always said that, in life, it's not what happens to you that makes your experience of it, it's how you respond and react to events that determines whether a time is good or bad. You can choose. *I* will *be happy*, I decided. *I* choose *to be happy. I do*.

Knickers, followed another thought.

I am soooooo not happy, agreed another part of me.

Not listening, not listening, I told myself.

'Are you OK, Jess?' asked Gran.

I nodded and smiled. 'Just remembering something Mum used to say,' I said.

'And what was that?' asked Gran.

'Oh, something about choosing, um, choosing to be happy . . . which is why you must go, Gran. I think if Mum was here now, she'd say go for it. I know she would.'

Gran nodded. 'I think she would too. She was

always a game girl, my Eleanor. Always up for an adventure.'

'Exactly,' I said. I knew Gran was right. I could almost hear Mum saying, 'Let her go, Jess.' I'd just have to make my own adventure here in London without Gran.

5
Girl talk

'Porchester Park's like a blooming ghost town,' said Pia as we got ready at my house to go up to Alisha's. It was a couple of nights after Gran had told me her news.

'I know. What's happened to everyone?' I asked. 'I thought this was going to be the place to be when people started arriving back.'

'All off to their holiday homes – skiing in France, Switzerland, North America or catching some sun in the Caribbean, Thailand or India.'

'Where do you think we should go, dwarlings?' asked Flo. 'Cabin in the snowy mountains, beach house by the sea—'

'Or Primark down the mall?' Meg interrupted.

'I think one should stay in London this year. Jetting off is so last decade, don't you think?' Pia replied in her posh Queen's voice.

'Deffo,' I said, copying her in my own posh voice as I attempted to straighten my hair with my GHDs. 'It's so common to travel when everyone else does, one thinks. But the Lewises will be here, won't they? I bet they'll make their apartment look fabbie and festive.'

'Actually, I'll be away,' said Flo. 'My family are going up to Scotland to see my grandparents.'

I sighed. 'Cross another one off the list, Pia,' I said. 'I suppose you'll be leaving us too, Meg?'

Meg looked sheepish. 'Actually, we were supposed to be staying in London but my granddad's not been well, so last night Mum said we're all off to Cornwall.'

'Blimey! I was joking!' I looked over at Pia. 'Please, please don't you tell me you're leaving.'

Pia grinned. 'No getting rid of me, matey.'

'Phew,' I said, although part of me knew that Pia had already gone in one way. She'd be hanging out with Henry more than me. Still, at least there would be JJ and Alisha.

I was making a special effort with my appearance before going upstairs in case JJ was there. Last time I'd seen him outside, I was freezing with a red nose. Not my best look. The only other times he saw me were when we swam together in the spa but then I'd be in my cossie with my hair scraped back. Also not my best look. Staff and their families aren't supposed to swim in the spa but I am allowed because when JJ had found out that I was a good swimmer, he had asked that I pace him. Permission had been granted straight away. What a resident wants, a resident gets in this place. Dad's motto is 'if a resident wants something and we haven't got it, we'll have it in twenty-four hours.'

'Working the system,' Charlie had commented when I told him. So far it had been great, apart from the fact that JJ never saw me dressed up. I wanted him to see me looking good.

'Alisha said she'd had some feedback from her mates in the States for our boy study,' I said as I applied a slick of lip gloss.

'Yeah,' said Pia. 'She's really got into it. When we first met her, I thought she was so confident and must have had loads of boyfriends and experience. It was nice to find out that she's just like us.'

'Me too,' said Meg, who was sitting on my bed and had adopted the yoga Lotus position much to Dave's bemusement. He kept trying to climb into her lap but couldn't get comfortable because of her up-turned feet. 'Just shows you can't assume anything by appearances, doesn't it?'

'We meet boys at school but she's home-schooled so where *would* she meet anyone she fancies?' said Pia. 'She can't go and hang out at the mall or the movies like we would. Everywhere she goes, her minder goes too. It must be hard for her.'

'I'd swap,' said Flo, as she fastened a silver Alice band in her hair. 'Ready, everyone?'

I nodded. 'JJ, prepare to fall under my spell,' I said to my reflection.

Pia laughed, stood up and did a cheerleader type dance. 'Go, Jess. Go, Jess. GO JESS, GO!'

I picked up my pillow and bopped her over the head with it. Violence is the only way to deal with Pia when she's having a manic attack.

The reception area twinkled festively as we passed through. To the left, on the mantelpiece over the fireplace, was a lush white bower hung with crystal icicles and white snowflakes, to the right, in an enormous frosted vase, were silver branches and around the hearth were candles which smelt of amber, orange and cinnamon. Jo Malone. They always were at Number 1.

'It's a shame there aren't going to be many people around to appreciate it,' I said as we stood and gazed at the scene for a few moments.

'*We* appreciate it,' said Meg. 'Stuff the richies.'

I laughed. She was right. Why was I worrying about who wasn't there to see it when I was?

Alisha came out to meet us in the hall of the Lewises' apartment and whisked us up to her bedroom before we had a chance to see how they'd decorated for Christmas. I didn't mind though, I love Alisha's bedroom. It's almost as big as the whole ground floor of our house and is decorated in shades of gold and ivory. On the wall above her bed is a larger than life portrait of her. It was taken by the famous Italian photographer, Alonzo de Cosima, and shows her in profile looking down at something in her lap. She looks so peaceful and thoughtful in it and it's beautifully lit, as if she's sitting by a window with the late afternoon sunshine pouring in and turning her skin to dark honey. She also has her own bathroom to the left and walk-in dressing room to the right. I tried not to be jealous the first time I saw it but it was hard not to be when I saw that she had a whole wall just for her shoes. She has every pair of Converse in every pattern and shade that they've ever made. On the other three walls, her clothes are hung according to colour: blue, black, white, red, pink. It's awesome. I have a tiny wardrobe from Ikea in the corner of my room and my clothes are shoved in there in an untidy mess. I dream of having a room like Alisha's where everything looks like it has just come back from the dry cleaners. Which it probably has.

'Been shopping?' asked Flo.

I followed Flo's gaze and saw that along one side of the room were designer carrier bags and a stack of parcels wrapped beautifully in expensive-looking paper with perfect ribbons and flowers. I spied some of the labels: Chanel, Cartier, Jo Malone, Tiffany, Gucci.

Alisha nodded. 'Presents. I got something for all of you.'

I glanced at Pia and she raised an eyebrow. I knew she got what I was thinking, what could we get for our rich mate that she couldn't buy a million of herself? I couldn't give her *another* music CD so what *could* I get her that would be special? The sort of things that the girls and I bought each other would seem pathetic to JJ and Alisha – a bar of strawberry-scented soap from the market just didn't measure up to Chanel or Dior, a pretty hair clip from Accessorise wasn't the same as one from Gucci or Prada.

I went and sat on the velvet chaise longue near the window and looked out. I would have to think of something original to give her, but what?

Way down below, I could see the homeless man in his usual doorway. He'd made an effort for Christmas and was wearing a Santa hat. *Weird*, I thought, *here's me up on top of the world in this luxury apartment, a place where the decorations in reception cost thousands and there's that man down there with nothing but a cardboard box*. The thought made me feel really uncomfortable.

'So, peeps, down to business,' said Alisha. 'My friends in LA have been brill at getting back with answers to your questions, Jess. They want your results too. Seems you're not the only girl out there who feels she has a lot to learn.'

'Cool,' I said. 'Maybe I should publish my findings as a book for other unfortunate girls! We could call it, *How to Be a Winner in Love* or something like that.'

'Good idea,' said Alisha. 'A friend of my dad's owns a publishing house in New York. I could take it to him.'

I'd been joking but I was learning fast that with the Lewis family and their connections, anything was possible. Visions of a glamorous launch party flooded my brain. Book signings. My face up on billboards over London, New York, Hong Kong. Talk shows. Jess Hall – boy expert. I could be an international celebrity and the paparazzi would be after me as much as the Porchester Park A-listers.

'Dad might not let me though,' said Alisha with a sigh. 'Probably not right for his image to have a daughter pushing a book on how to get a boy. Sometimes being me sucks. Everything I do, I have to think how it might reflect back on Dad.'

'Ditto,' I said.

Alisha gave me a quizzical look.

'Not *your* dad, dozo,' I said. 'Mine. Since we moved here, I have to be ultra well-behaved in case I do anything that reflects badly on Porchester Park.'

'She had to give up being a pole dancer *and* a drug dealer,' said Pia in a solemn voice.

Alisha laughed. 'Me too,' she said and joined the palm of her hands in the prayer position. 'Now I'm as pure as snow. Sadly always was. I've never had the chance to really misbehave. If I tried, there would always be someone watching me – like a minder.'

'I have a feeling that Riko Mori feels like that,' I said. 'I saw her checking out the exits the other day.'

'Yeah,' said Alisha. 'To us, a day just cruising the shops without anyone chaperoning us would be heaven. Maybe she's lonely, like I was when I first got here. If all her mates are at school, who's she supposed to hang out with over the holidays?'

'I hadn't thought about that. Maybe we should include her when we do things?' I said.

'I would, but she's not very friendly,' said Alisha. 'I saw her in the lobby the other day and tried to start a conversation but she wasn't interested.'

Pia shrugged. 'Maybe she was fed up. Holidays without a mate are no fun at all. Maybe she'll have some insight about boys to share. She looks pretty cool. I bet she's sussed about them. We should ask her.'

'What did your friends in the States say, Alisha?' I asked.

Alisha got up and went to her computer. 'Lots,' she

said as she found the page she wanted. 'Casey says that you just have to be yourself with them. She asked her brother what he thought and he said he likes girls who are natural and don't try too hard.'

'Easier said than done,' I said. 'I agree with her but if I like a boy, I go stupid and although I'd like to be myself, I can't be, I get nervous and act like I have no brain.'

'That's because you don't,' said Pia.

I ignored her.

'You have to chill,' said Alisha. 'Remember, boys can get nervous too, so they might not even notice that you're ill at ease.'

'I guess,' I said and I told myself that if I saw JJ later, I would relax and be myself.

'What none of you realise,' said Pia, 'is that we are *girls*. That alone is enough for most boys. Show a bit of cleavage, have shiny hair, smell lovely and they are putty in your hands.'

'Yeah, but I don't want a boy to like me because of my body or my looks. I want a boy to like me for *me*,' said Meg.

'Pia's right though,' I said. 'I read somewhere that boys are primarily visual. If they like what they see, then they'll make an effort to get to know you.'

'That's so shallow,' said Meg.

'Not really. We're the same, aren't we?' I asked. 'Like, would you snog Jacob West?' Meg pulled a face. 'Exactly. And he's really a nice guy so why don't you get to know him. He can't help the fact he looks like a potato with ears.'

Alisha cracked up laughing. 'I think Jess is right. We have to make the effort, girls. Lure them in by being bee-ootiful. Any girl can be with a good haircut, a bit of lip gloss and a pair of great shades.'

'Easy for you with a hairdresser, manicurist and stylist on hand – not to mention wardrobes of designer clothes,' I said.

'Money can't buy style, guys. Some girls I knew back home had a ton of money but never looked the biz. Other girls looked great because they had attitude and confidence.'

'That's true,' said Pia and she lay back on the bed Cleopatra-style. 'I don't have the dosh but I *do* know how to put together a look.' She did too. She had a great eye for colour and knew how to finish an outfit off with the right jewellery.

'Style can't always be bought,' I said. 'It's being creative. I love what Riko wears, it's insane but it works.'

'It works because she works it. She's confident. I

know this sounds all LA-speak again,' said Alisha and she stuck her tongue out at me, 'but tough, I'm gonna say it anyway, it's not just the clothes, it's attitude. If you walk tall and are confident, people will respond to that. Act like a loser and put that out and people will pick up on it. Why wouldn't they?'

Pia looked pointedly at me. 'Exactly,' she said with a nod.

'Hard for me to walk tall at my height,' said Meg. 'But I get what you're saying.'

'I wish I could be more confident and give it some attitude,' I said, 'but I'm totally rubbish at the whole thing. I like Tom. I *think* he likes me but he's also a player, so I'm not sure he's interested in having a proper girlfriend.'

'And Charlie hardly even knows I exist,' said Flo, looking up from the glossy magazine she'd had her nose in since we got up to Alisha's room.

'Ah,' said Alisha. 'So move on. I know I haven't had much experience but I think you should find a boy who isn't going to mess with your head. Thing is, sometimes if a boy is really good-looking, like Tom is, then they know they can get away with playing the field – but not all boys are like him, some do want a steady relationship. Like my brother JJ: he's nice-looking but he doesn't mess girls around. He'd rather be with one girl that he can get to know than a different girl every night.'

Pia grinned like an idiot and looked pointedly at me again. I went bright red. Subtle is not a word in Pia's vocabulary and I wondered if Alisha had guessed that I liked JJ. Luckily, she didn't seem to notice my blushing.

'And Flo,' Alisha continued, 'I reckon you should let Charlie know you like him.'

'Oh, he knows,' said Flo. 'He just chooses to ignore it.'

'He's more into music and hanging with his mates,' I explained and Flo sighed. 'Girls just aren't high up on his list.'

'Maybe I should learn how to play the guitar,' she said.

'Not a bad idea,' said Meg. 'You write great poetry. Why don't you write some lyrics and send them to him?'

'I think boys like Tom, who get off with loads of girls, are trying to prove something. They're just insecure,' said Pia.

'I hardly think Tom is insecure,' I said. 'He's a natural babe magnet. What else did your friends say, Alisha?'

'One said that it's a good idea when you want to break up with a boy to lie about how strict your parents are. You can use your mum or dad as your reason for breaking up, like – Dad says I have to cool it because I have to knuckle down and study for my exams, or Mum says I'm too young to be in a serious relationship.'

'But that's a cop-out,' said Pia. 'Why not just tell the truth?'

'Yeah. All very well if you have a boyfriend to break-up *with*,' I said and Flo nodded.

'We'll get there,' said Alisha. 'She also said those excuses only work when followed by a boy-free period, not if you dive straight into the arms of another boy.'

'Sounds like your friends have a lot more experience that we do,' I said. '*Another* boy? It took me ages to meet one boy I like, never mind think about another one.'

Out of Alisha's eyeline, Pia held up two fingers and silently mouthed, 'Two boys. You like *two* boys.'

I ignored her again.

'Yeah, but it's still good advice not to break up with

one boy and start snogging his best friend in the vicinity of the broken-hearted old boyfriend and vice versa,' said Meg. 'That's what my sister did last year and she really hurt the first boy. She said it was was very difficult to behave when her hormones were raging. She said that hormones and lust can lead girls astray and cause them to forget their manners. Just like boys. I think she's just a slut.'

I laughed. I'd met Meg's sister. She's the total opposite of Meg, a curvy girlie blonde who lives for boys and usually has a new one each week.

'We should add that to your list of questions, Jess,' said Flo. 'We've been so busy thinking about how to get a boy to notice us, we haven't even thought forward to how to break-up with one if we don't get on.'

'A swift karate chop to the neck would do it, I reckon,' said Meg. We all cracked up. I *think* she was joking.

I made a note of the question to be added. What *is* the best way to break up with a boy?

Alisha suggested that we went down the kitchen to get snacks and drinks so we all trooped after her.

'Someone going somewhere?' asked Pia, when she saw a suitcase in the hall.

Alisha looked at the case. 'Yes and no. That belongs to Carly. She just got here from the States.'

'Carly?' I asked, as we went into the vast marble kitchen where JJ was sitting at the breakfast bar sipping a Coke and flicking through a magazine. It's a fab room. A huge American fridge freezer, that I knew from previous visits holds every type of juice imaginable plus a range of other yummy-looking goodies; an enormous range cooker; gleaming surfaces and a glass wall at the end with a view over Hyde Park.

JJ looked up. 'Hey girls.'

'Hey JJ,' we chorused.

'Where's Carly?' asked Alisha.

JJ indicated the cloakroom to the left.

'JJ's girlfriend,' whispered Alisha, 'they were sweethearts back home. She's come to spend Christmas with us.'

Girlfriend! I thought, as my heart sank. *Since when did JJ have a girlfriend? God, this Christmas is just getting worse and worse.*

A beautiful girl appeared moments later and Alisha did the introductions. She was perfect: perfectly straight white-blonde hair; a slim perfect body in an immaculate white T-shirt and jeans; flawless skin; a perfect smile that showed perfectly even white teeth. She looked like she'd been cracked out of styrofoam that morning. With my hair that refused to stay straight, my old jeans and scruffy blue shirt, I couldn't hope to compete. It all clicked into place in a nano second. So *this* was who JJ had meant when he'd said he was going to spend Christmas with someone special. He'd never meant *me* at all. How could I have even thought that for a second? *I am so hopeless at reading boys*, I thought as I fixed a smile on my face in an attempt to hide my disappointment. *First Tom and now JJ. Once again I take the prize. Love loser of the year.*

'Hi Carly,' said Pia. 'Welcome to London.'

'Thanks. Hey, great to meet you all,' she said in an American accent and with a big smile.

'Staying long?' Pia asked and I knew she was asking for me.

Carly looked coyly at JJ. 'Not really. Just passing through. I was in Italy but Mr Lewis invited me to spend Christmas with the family in Aspen.'

'Aspen?' I asked.

Alisha nodded. 'All very last minute. Dad didn't think he'd be able to make it but he really needs a break so we're all off to Colorado until the New Year. Skiing!'

Pia gave my arm a squeeze. She knew how I'd be feeling about JJ and on top of that, Alisha was jetting off too. Sometimes it was hard being friends with someone who wasn't just loaded, but mega-loaded. There was no way I could keep up. I didn't even know where Aspen was, to me it sounded like a breakfast cereal.

When we trooped back up to Alisha's bedroom later, I felt flat and confused. I didn't like how I was feeling. It was like when I'd first moved in to Porchester Park, the whole issue of them and us. I'd been pretty mixed up about it then. I'd hoped that I'd moved on, but nope, those old feelings were back and they'd brought a bunch of friends.

6
Only the lonely

The Lewis family left two days later. The Russian family went the same day, before I even got a chance to check out Alexei. Loads of other residents were also seen disappearing in fleets of limos, heading for the airport. It was a grand exodus from Porchester Park. Gran, Meg and Flo included. All off to their fabbie-dabbie locations around the world.

Pia was still around but, as I'd suspected, I hardly saw her any more, nor Henry. Even Charlie commented that Henry hadn't been round as much as usual. Pia asked me to go to a movie with them one night but I knew she'd prefer to be on her own with him. No way was I going to sit with them like a sad hanger on. *So much for my Christmas plans*, I thought. *No Tom, no JJ, no Gran, no new teenagers to meet, no Flo, Meg, Alisha or Pia.* I went round our house singing the Celine Dion number, *All by myself*, until Charlie told me to shut up and get a life. He wasn't around much either. He was in a band and was always off rehearsing. Tom sometimes played with them too and I knew that Charlie had seen him a few times but no matter how hard I tried to chisel information out of him, he wasn't giving much away – either that or they didn't talk about girls.

'How's Tom?' I persisted over breakfast, the week before Christmas Day.

He shrugged his left shoulder.

'Is he seeing anyone?'

He shrugged the other shoulder.

'Has he got a girlfriend?'

He gave me a blank look. 'Dunno.'

'So what *do* you talk about when you get together?'

'Music.'

'Don't you ever talk about girls or relationships?'

'Nope.'

Boys are so different to girls, I thought. With my mates, I know within five minutes exactly how they are, what they're feeling, their latest crushes, all the intimate details of their lives, but boys never seem to know what's going on in their friends' heads.

I turned to Dad. 'I despair. Why didn't you and Mum have another girl so I could have a sister to talk to? All my mates are busy. Everyone's going away and I'm *lonely*.'

'How can you be lonely when you're in one of the most exciting cities in the world with a thousand things going on?' said Dad as his phone rang.

'Ah, but a person can still be lonely in a crowd,' I replied. I thought that was very deep but Dad just rolled his eyes, took the call then said, 'Your Aunt Maddie's at the gate. Go and let her in.'

No-one understands me, I thought as I got up to do as I was told. Aunt Maddie, the Scroogemeister, my only company for the hols. Could it *get* any worse?

Five minutes later, Aunt Maddie was unpacking bags in the kitchen. I noticed that Dad had quickly made himself scarce. He's not daft. Aunt M can be heavy going sometimes. She gets intense about things, like saving the world, going green or recycling. Whichever, you could always guarantee a lecture on something worthy.

'A few presents for your Christmas tree,' she said as she unpacked parcels wrapped in red and gold, which was unusual for her. She didn't normally do wrapping paper, what with the season being a commercial venture in her eyes. I wondered what she'd got us this year – probably something festive like a book with the title *Save the Turkey, he has a soul* or *How to make your own soap from leftover parsnips*.

Aunt Maddie was Mum's younger sister and about as different to Mum as anyone could be. Mum'd had style. Aunt Maddie went out of her way to dress like a bag lady, in jeans that sagged around the bottom and fleeces that sagged around the top. Today she was wearing a strange woolly green hat with earflaps. Not a good look. Sometimes I wondered what it had been like for her growing up with Mum. *It must have been hard having a prettier, funnier sister who everyone loved*, I thought. Suddenly I felt kinder towards Aunt M. I knew all about being the one left out.

'Will you be spending Christmas with Brian?' I asked.

Brian was her boyfriend and largely responsible for the change in her. Although she'd always been intense, she'd grown even more so after meeting him.

He really was Mr Do Good, Go Green, Save the World, Killjoy. The first time I met him, he'd given me a talking to about wearing make-up and what a waste of time it was.

Aunt Maddie shook her head. 'We broke up.'

'Broke up! But why? You seemed so right for each other.'

Aunt Maddie looked sad. 'He found someone else. A twenty-year-old someone else.'

'Are you OK?'

She shrugged like it didn't matter but I could see by the shadows under her eyes that it did.

'I won't be seeing the boys I like, either,' I said, in an attempt to make her feel better.

She laughed. 'Boys? Not just one?'

'I was keeping my options open but well . . . neither of them worked out. In fact, I've realised I don't know a lot about boys at all. I mean how are you supposed to find out? Having an older brother doesn't help. All he does is grunt at me these days. I'm doing some personal research into the whole boy/girl thing, hoping that I can learn something to pass on to other ignorant girls like me. Have you got any pearls of wisdom to share about them?'

Aunt Maddie thought for a moment. 'Just think of

a boy, or a man, as a big daft dog with attention-deficit disorder and you won't go far wrong.'

Now it was my turn to laugh. 'Seriously?'

Aunt Maddie nodded. 'It took me years to work that one out. Most men are boys at heart, even the forty- or fifty-year-old ones. We ladies credit them with far too much intelligence and sensitivity, whereas most of them are just looking for their mum.'

'Isn't that sexist?' I'd never heard Aunt Maddie talk like this before. Brian really had hurt her.

'Maybe. I don't care. The biggest mistake a girl can ever make, Jess, is to expect a boy to fulfill everything. They can't. We girls must get a life, use our brains, be independent and not become doormats.'

'I can't imagine you ever becoming a doormat,' I said.

'Me neither but love makes you behave in strange ways. I tried to be what I thought Brian wanted me to be. I should have just been myself.'

'That's what my mate says. Be yourself. But other friends say you have to make an effort – that boys are visual and have to like what they see,' I said as I looked pointedly at her baggy jeans.

'Pff,' said Aunt Maddie. 'Men are quite capable of falling in love with plain girls as well as beautiful ones, although . . . the girl Brian went off with *was* very pretty.'

'Even plain girls can look the biz,' I said, 'with the right hair and make-up. Anyway, you're not plain, in fact, you could be very pretty, Aunt Maddie. Why don't you let me do a makeover on you?'

Oops. Wrong thing to say. Lecture coming. I could tell by the way her back stiffened and her lips pursed together. I'd obviously hit a nerve.

'Wishing you're better-looking is probably the biggest teenage angst there is,' she said, 'even when people say you look lovely, you don't believe them. There's always someone better-looking, an image in a magazine you want to be like. It's a shallow world, Jess. Don't get stuck in it. It should be about who you are, not what you look like.'

So I was right, I thought. She could never live up to my mum and her response was to give up.

'I agree, Aunt Maddie, but I think there has to be a balance. Yes, be yourself but wear a bit of lip gloss while you're doing it.'

Aunt Maddie cracked up. It was good to see her laugh and it made me realise I hadn't seen her do so for quite some time.

'Sometimes you're just like your mum, Jess.'

I liked the sound of that. I smiled. 'So, what will you do at Christmas?' I asked.

'I'm organising Christmas lunch for the homeless,' she said. 'It's at the Guild Hall school. We'll be catering for two hundred. What are you doing?'

'Ah. Um. I'm here. Catering for three.'

'Like to come and help out? It can be great fun.'

'Fun? No way,' I blurted. I couldn't help it. Christmas Day with the down-and-outs was so *not* on my wish list.

'What else are you going to do?'

'Well, exactly,' I said crossly. 'All my plans have been scuppered so I suppose I might as well come and join the great unwashed and unwanted.'

'Jess, that's no way to talk about them. If you heard some of their stories, it would break your heart. People who've lost their families, businesses, fortunes, homes. Most of them didn't *choose* to be homeless you know, any more than you chose for Gran to change her plans. Sometimes life deals you a round of bad cards.'

'Tell me about it. Now I feel guilty too,' I said. 'Thanks a bunch. Deck the halls with Christmas holly, tis the season to be *jolly*, you know, not slave away serving up lunch to people you don't know.'

'Exactly. But why shouldn't the homeless be jolly too? They have nothing in their lives but the clothes they stand up in and they don't always have those! It wouldn't hurt you to come and give up some of your time. You live a privileged life, Jess. I do too. I have a home, heating, food on the table. Sometimes we should give something back.'

I felt like I'd swallowed a stone. There was no getting out of it. I didn't exactly have any plans I couldn't break but why should it be *me* having to give something back when other people swanned off to their holiday homes in the sun? Why was I the one with an Aunt Maddie, conscience of the blooming world? Why meeeeeeeeee?

'Tell you what. You come with me and help out on December twenty-fifth and later we can have our Christmas celebration. Mum will be back from Florence just after New Year and she'll do a big dinner with all the trimmings then. It doesn't matter what date it happens. What are you going to do this week?'

'Nothing. Everyone's away and Pia's got a boyfriend.'

'Ah. But that shouldn't stop you. London's a great place to be during the Christmas run up.'

'That's what Dad said.'

'He's right. There are outdoor ice-skating rinks, carol services all over the place, window displays to look at in all the big shops, shows, movies, loads of things to do.'

'And all are more fun if you have someone to do them with.'

'Tell Pia that you're feeling left out. If I know her, she'll be round in an instant.'

I knew Aunt Maddie was right but I was finding it hard to shake off the blues. Sometimes I think that feelings are like clothes and some days, you wake up and just find you're wearing them. Today, I was swathed in stubborn and sulky. 'Christmas was always something Mum did. We had our traditions and now we have nothing.'

Aunt Maddie's expression softened. 'I know, love. But who started those traditions? She did, and some of them you can carry on but why not start a few of your own, too? Think about what *you'd* like to do, places you'd like to go, people you'd like to spend time with. Life is what you make of it, you know.'

'I guess. When life throws you lemons, make lemonade. Mum used to say that. I have my own saying and that is when life throws you a lemon, duck . . . or throw it back.'

'That's not the Jess I know. You would never duck. Come on. Take a challenge. Do something different. Christmas Day with the homeless. What do you say?'

I felt I couldn't say no without being the worst person in the world. 'I suppose I have to now,' I said and then an idea occurred to me. 'But seeing as I don't really want to and you're blackmailing me through guilt . . . how about we do a deal?'

Aunt Maddie looked at me suspiciously. 'Do a deal?'

'I do something I don't want to. You do something you don't want to.'

Aunt Maddie narrowed her eyes. 'I've got a feeling I'm not going to like this, but go on. What's the deal?'

'You let me do a makeover on you.'

Aunt Maddie sighed heavily and I thought I'd let myself in for another lecture but then she smiled and held out her hand to shake. 'Fair enough,' she said. 'Deal.'

When it was time for her to go, I walked with Aunt Maddie to her bus-stop then made my way to our local shop to buy some milk. It was freezing outside, with a bitter wind and, on the way back, I noticed

Bridget over in the usual paparazzi spot looking pale with cold. I nodded at her when I went past.

'OK, Jess?' she asked.

'Yeah. You look frozen.'

She nodded, her teeth chattering. 'Part of the job,' she said. 'So glamorous, don't you think? We get to go to all the best locations.'

I laughed. It wouldn't do any harm to chat to her for a few moments. 'What's it really like being a journalist, Bridget?'

'Hard work, long hours, waiting in all weathers for the big scoop,' she said then indicated the few others who were parked nearby, stomping their feet and hugging themselves to keep warm. 'And very competitive.'

'So why don't you do some other kind of writing?'

'And that's not competitive? Believe me, I have my novel on the go. Me and twenty thousand others.'

'Don't you feel bad invading people's privacy?'

'Ah now, the paper I work for doesn't set out to ruin anyone's reputation, unlike some who print what they like. I'm looking for the interesting story, so I am. People these days are fascinated by celebrity, so I go where the trend is. Like anyone else, I have bills to pay, I have to make a living.'

'But who are you hoping to see come in or out of Porchester Park?' I asked. 'Most people have gone away to their holiday homes. It's almost empty.'

'Must be quiet for you in there, then,' Bridget asked.

'Ghost town,' I said.

'What's it like living there for you?'

I looked at her suspiciously. 'Hey, you're not catching me out.'

'Not angling for a story, angel. I'm just interested. I mean, there's a lot of people with a lot of money in there . . .'

'And I'm ordinary. Is that what you were going to say?'

'Not ordinary, Jess. *Normal*. You and your brother live a normal life. Back and forth to school. I see you getting off the bus as they get out of limos. You must note the contrast on many levels.'

I nodded. I felt like I'd already said too much but it was nice to be asked about me for a change and it seemed like she was just chatting, not digging for dirt. All the same, I didn't want to get into trouble. 'Better be going in now, Bridget.'

'Sure. And have a lovely Christmas.'

'You too,' I replied.

She's OK, I thought as I let myself back through the side gate. *Paparazzi are only human after all*.

When I got back up to my room, I called Pia. 'A-*allllll byyyy my-se-el-elelf*,' I warbled into the phone. '*I don't wanna be . . .*'

Pia laughed at the other end. 'Gotcha,' she said. 'Actually, I was thinking I'd been neglecting you lately. Sorry. Bad friend. I forgot the golden rule. Mates first, boys second.'

'So, do you want to hang out and do Christmas London-style?'

7
It's Christmas!

'Don't ever let it be said that I haven't given this Christmas my best,' I said to the photo of Mum that I kept in my bedroom.

In the last week, I'd taken Aunt Maddie and Dad's advice and packed in as many Christmassy things as I could.

Pia and I had been to see the lights on Oxford Street. Oo, lover-ly.

Charlie, Henry, Pia and me had been ice-skating on the outdoor rink up on Hampstead Heath. Oops, only fell over three times.

I'd been to Trafalgar Square to see the tree and

sung along with the carol service that was going on. Ding dong merrily on hi-i-i-igh.

I'd been to Selfridges to meet Santa in his grotto but felt a bit daft lining up with a bunch of three-year-olds so went and tried all the perfumes on the ground floor instead. Mmmm. Nice.

Pia and I had got the boat from Westminster down to Greenwich and got most of our presents from the indoor market there. Handmade soap for Flo and Meg. Music CDs for Charlie, a fab brown velvet hat for Aunt Maddie to replace the monstrosity with ear-flaps that she wears which looks like a tea-cosy. It probably *is* a tea cosy. A book on history for Dad – if he ever has time to read it – and a green silk scarf for Pia when she was off buying chips.

Me and Pia even went to the Great Christmas Pudding Race in Covent Garden, which is a mad affair where people run around balancing a pudding on a plate whilst crowds of spectators try to grab, jostle and trip them up. There was a great atmosphere there. Near the Piazza, a vintage carousel was a whirl of brass and chrome as children rode the beautifully carved horses and called out to each other over the carols that wheezed out from an ancient-sounding organ. Everywhere, endless stalls offered a multitude of gifts for shoppers eagerly looking for stocking fillers. Busking musicians sang festive songs, street performers juggled, danced and did astonishing acrobatics, while mime artists dressed as robots, aliens and characters from history stood as still as statues.

Lastly, I went to Sadler's Wells to see the Nutcracker ballet with Pia and her mum. It was truly magical and Pia and I pirouetted all the way back to the tube. All good fun, all very merry but I couldn't help but notice the couples everywhere we went. Misty-eyed, arm-in-arm, laden with parcels, laughing together, living out *my* Christmas fantasies – only I had no boy to play them out with. Boo hoo, sob sob. Poor moi.

'It's a strange time,' I said to Pia as we stuffed ourselves with croissants at her house on Christmas Eve morning. 'Like, there's this huge pressure on us all to be happy because it's Christmas. You *must* be happy, have a jolly time, but what if you don't feel like that? Mrs Moran was right. There *is* a lot to think about.'

Pia slurped a glass of orange juice. 'Yeah. What makes your ding dong merrily on high? Different things for different people.'

'When Mum was alive, it was always about *our* traditions. Things we did every year that made it Christmas for us.'

'I know. So why not make some of the things we've done this week your new tradition?'

I screwed up my face. 'Maybe.' I thought over the things we'd done but none of them seemed enough. My mum was special and I needed something unique to remember her by. 'But what? I'd like to do something that I know she would have loved but also something different. Apart from going to see the tree in Trafalgar Square, which was cool, I can't say there's anything that felt like the right thing to commemorate her by.'

'So what *would* you like to do?' she asked.

'Dunno. Maybe I should go somewhere quiet, away from the rush and the shopping and people. Somewhere that feels, I don't know, sacred. A church, I think, maybe – maybe not – or a temple or mosque. I don't know what I believe yet and Mum wasn't religious either, although she always respected other people's beliefs. What I'm looking for is hard to describe, a kind of . . . inner calm. Do you know what I mean?'

Pia nodded and made a peace sign. 'Yeah, like

something with a good vibe, man. Yeah, I get you. That would be nice. Jess goes holy-moley.'

'Somewhere I can go or something I can do every Christmas to remember Mum.'

'That would be Westfield Mall, then,' said Pia with a grin. 'Right in the middle of the Marks and Spencer's food department. She loved the shops at Christmas. She loved people, feeding them, remember? Anyone who didn't have anywhere to go was welcome at your house.'

'What about a service at St Paul's or Westminster Abbey? I bet that would feel special,' I suggested.

'Maybe. Bit grown up, though. Your mum liked fun at Christmas. I think she'd like the carol singing in Trafalgar Square best.'

'Yeah. Maybe.' I didn't feel enthusiastic enough about any of the things we'd done to make them my new tradition, even though we'd had a good time exploring the options. Plus, I was dreading Christmas Day. While we'd been out and about in the last few days, I'd been super aware of the homeless. They made me feel uncomfortable with their hands held out for money, looking and smelling like they needed a good bath. And I felt guilty about them being on the streets when I had a warm home to go back to.

Even so, I wasn't looking forward to having to spend a whole afternoon with them.

I woke the next morning with a sinking feeling in my stomach. So much for ding dong merrily on high. This was going to be my most miserable Christmas Day ever, though at least Charlie had agreed to come to the lunch as well.

'No way I'm staying here on my own,' he said as we made our way on foot to the lunch location in West London. Aunt Maddie had sent us a map and we worked out that we could walk there in twenty minutes or so. Luckily the day was dry and bright as we trudged along. I couldn't help but notice cars full of smiling faces, no doubt on their way to some scrummy lunch with family and friends somewhere. *Bah humbug*, I thought. *Grrrr*.

'I reckon we go in, do our bit, then get out,' I said. 'This is so not what I want to be doing today. I want to get back as soon as possible, put my feet up on the sofa, turn the telly on, and open a box of chocs.'

'It'll be fine,' said Charlie. That was his attitude to most things. He cruised through life in a bubble and rarely got worked up about anything.

*

The Victorian building where the event was to be held felt cold and smelt of wet concrete. It was already filling up by the time we got inside and I stared at the odd bunch of people taking their places in the main hall. Some seemed to know each other but I noticed a few on their own, sitting in corners, nervously eyeing the proceedings. A few of them hardly looked older than me and Charlie.

'What are those teenagers doing here?' I asked Aunt Maddie when she came out to greet us, then led us to the kitchens.

'Everyone has their story,' she replied. 'Some have run away from violent or abusive parents. Some have got into drugs and been disowned. All sorts of stories.'

'Why don't they get jobs?' asked Charlie.

'Ah,' said Aunt Maddie. 'Easy to say. That's what everyone asks but if you haven't got an address or a bank account, it's hard to get employment. Some of the older folk are here because they were made redundant then couldn't keep up with their rent or bills so lost their homes. Some are alcoholics whose habit has caused them to lose their family or home. No home address, no job. No job, no way of paying your rent. It's a vicious circle.'

'Wow. That's tough,' said Charlie.

Aunt Maddie nodded. 'It is. Believe me, the majority of these people don't want to be in this position. There are experts here today who can advise them, though, maybe help them get back to having a normal life. In fact, there are all sorts of volunteers on hand here: doctors, dentists, opticians, counsellors, all kinds of medical help – because that's another thing that goes with your home, with no address to register with a doctor, they can't just walk in and be seen. For the three days they come here, there's a chance to seek advice, have a hot shower, even a haircut – all the things we take for granted.'

We spent the next hour preparing vegetables and generally helping out in the kitchen. Apart from having to wear a kind of shower cap to keep my hair out of the food, it wasn't as bad as I'd imagined it would be. The volunteers were a jolly bunch and one of them started a round of Christmas carols. Soon everyone in the place was singing their heads off as we peeled carrots and prepared a mountain of sprouts.

'Go and take a break,' said Aunt Maddie once most of the lunch was ready and the kitchen was beginning to smell of roast turkey. 'Go and see what's happening.'

I didn't want to go out and mix with the homeless. I wouldn't know what to say to them, so I busied myself clearing our chopping area.

Aunt Maddie must have seen my reticence. 'They won't bite,' she said. 'Go and explore. There's a lot going on.'

She pushed me gently in the direction of the door to the main hall and Charlie took off his hat and apron and came with me. A bunch of sad people getting dental checks and haircuts wasn't high on my agenda as a fun thing to do on Christmas Day. I'd rather have stayed in the kitchen but I felt bad even thinking that. I felt sorry for the homeless but I felt awkward about having to go out and talk to them. *It's weird*, I thought, *days ago I was thinking I couldn't keep up with my rich friends at Porchester Park and how they're from a different world and today I feel as if* I'm *in a different world to the people here. It's weird how some people have so much, some people so little.*

In the main hall, I was surprised to see a rock band of fit boys about Charlie's age entertaining the waiting diners. In another room, behind the main area, a trio of musicians were playing classical music on a cello, violin and harp. The audience in there was made up of older people, some sitting with their eyes closed, enjoying the music and probably the warmth of being inside. I noticed one man had a tatty pair of sandals on. *Must be freezing for him in winter without proper shoes*, I thought, as we went back into the corridor where a magician was moving amongst everyone, doing tricks. We stopped to watch him for a while and oo-ed and ah-ed with the others as he brought pound coins out of thin air.

'Could you teach me how to do that?' asked an old man seated on his own by the entrance. He looked like anyone's granddad with ruddy cheeks, white hair and kindly eyes but there was an air of sadness about him, apparent from his shabby clothes, his stooped posture and his weary expression.

'That's Arthur,' said Aunt Maddie, coming up behind me and drawing me to one side. 'He's a dear.'

'Why's he here?' I asked.

'He lost his wife a few years back and had a mental breakdown. They'd been together since they were teenagers and he couldn't cope without her. He just fell apart, lost his job and then his house was taken away.'

'And he has nowhere to go?'

Aunt Maddie shook her head. 'At least he can come here for a few days, but it's not enough.'

'No,' I agreed.

Charlie indicated a man at the far end of the corridor who had a puppy on his lap. 'A lot of them have dogs,' he said. 'Why's that?'

'They don't have anyone else. No home, no friends – just their dog. Sometimes, they'll feed their animal before themselves. I remember once seeing a man out in the rain with his dog and the dog was in his sleeping bag, wearing a rain-hat, whilst his owner got soaked!'

'I can understand that,' I said. 'Animals love you unconditionally. You'll never find a more loyal friend.' I was thinking of my cat, Dave. I'd had him since he was a kitten and, apart from Pia, he was my best friend – always there for a cuddle, my constant companion on the end of my bed when I woke up and when I went to sleep. After Mum died, I'd felt he'd understood how sad I was and made a special effort to be near to me and unlike with humans, I didn't have to put on a brave act or even talk to him.

'Exactly,' said Aunt Maddie. 'These people are just like us. They have feelings and they need companionship. Some of the centres don't let dogs in over Christmas but we do. We recognise what they mean to our guests.'

I liked that and I was beginning to change my view of the homeless. A sudden fracas broke out in one room and within seconds, two burly men passed us holding on to a dishevelled man with shoulder-length ratty hair. As they passed, we stepped back and pressed ourselves against the wall. He stank really badly, plus I could smell alcohol as they went by, the man shouting and swearing at everyone.

'Not all our guests are sweethearts like Arthur,' said Aunt Maddie as the man was escorted firmly out of the front door. 'Some are angry, bitter, difficult. No doubt that man has his story too but we have a zero-tolerance policy about bad behaviour here. We have to, because a few people can ruin things for everyone else and that wouldn't be fair.'

Aunt Maddie then showed us the dormitories in the back halls where up to fifty people would sleep.

'We can't house everyone here,' she said as we looked at the narrow beds lined up along the walls, 'but there are six centres open like this around the city and over three thousand volunteers working. At least we can get some of them off the streets, if only for a short time.'

'I hope Arthur has a bed,' I said.

'I already made sure he does,' said Aunt Maddie.

'He's one of my favourites. I wish I could do more for him but there are so many like him to help. But there are people here to give advice on housing, how to get benefits and how to get set up again.' She indicated an Indian lady in a corner with a couple of other older women. 'That's Usha over there. She was a teacher in a top school when she lived in India. Very proud. She despises her situation, being regarded as homeless. With her is Katya, a fantastic artist, and Sharon, a graduate who acts as quiz master for us every year. Many homeless people are actually highly qualified, some more so than the volunteers. There are ex-lawyers, ex-university lecturers, ex-teachers. All people who've had bad luck somewhere along the way.'

I looked into one room where there were a couple of teenage boys playing table tennis. 'What about that guy there?' I asked as we watched a fit-looking black boy thrash his opponent.

'That's Michael. He was thrown out by his parents when they found out he was gay. Not all societies are as liberal as the majority these days. In some ethnic groups being gay is still taboo.'

As we explored further, I was amazed at how many people there were about my or Charlie's age.

'There are more than a hundred and twenty thousand children and teens homeless or in temporary accommodation,' said Aunt Maddie when I asked about them. I glanced at some of their faces as we went through the various rooms. They looked no different to the kids at my school – hanging out, watching DVDs, playing cards – they just looked scruffier and maybe more tired, with shadows under their eyes. I couldn't imagine not having a bed and a hot shower each night and clean clothes every morning, and my heart went out to them. *I will never think of them just as the homeless again*, I thought, *I will think of them as people, just like me, but who have fallen on hard times. Individuals. I will remember each has their own story and I will think about who they are and* why *they have no home, instead of just thinking about them as people to be avoided.*

Soon it was time for lunch to be served in a hall where trestle tables had been laid out with red tablecloths, cutlery, glasses and crackers. Charlie and I helped serve up and I made sure I gave Arthur and Michael an extra helping of turkey. The atmosphere in the hall was happy and festive, with a great fuss made over the pulling of the crackers. Now everyone wore their paper hats, homeless and volunteers alike.

And not a scrap of food was left on the plates when we cleared away.

After lunch, I got chatting to a few of the guests, as Aunt Maddie called them. Mary, a young pregnant woman, cried when she told me that apart from having no home, she was anxious that the authorities would take her baby away. She also told me that the streets weren't safe for women. I couldn't imagine being out all night, in all weathers. I always hurried home when I had been out somewhere and always made sure I was with someone or had Dad or Gran pick me up if I was going to be late. It had been drilled into me by Mum, Gran and Dad that it wasn't safe to be out alone, but these girls were out all hours, on their own and vulnerable.

As I went around, I noticed that many of the guests had carrier bags with them. A cute cherub-faced volunteer called Matt told me that those bags contained all they owned in the world. I couldn't help thinking of Alisha's designer carrier bags stuffed with expensive presents, her dressing room full of more clothes than she could possibly wear. It was such a contrast.

'Sadly, lots of them turn to drugs and alcohol,' said Matt. 'I suppose it's a way to numb the reality of their situation and who can blame them? So many are depressed, feeling they have no hope so they drink themselves into oblivion to blot it all out. It's a downward spiral. If you're an alcoholic, no-one will employ you. If no-one will employ you, you get depressed, so you drink.'

'No wonder,' I said. 'It must be awful.'

The day so far had been a total wake-up call for me. Not what I'd expected at all. Yes, the situation was sad for all of them, but so many of them were brave and resigned and eager to get back to normal – and very enthusiastic about making the most of the facilities provided for these few days.

Charlie and I went back into the kitchens to do our share of the washing up then Aunt Maddie said that we could go home.

'You've both worked hard,' she said. 'Take off any time you want.'

I looked at Charlie. 'I'd like to stay. How about you?'

'Deffo,' he said. 'Anyway, I've a table tennis game booked with Michael.'

'Great,' I said, 'because Katya was going to show me some of her drawings.'

At tea-time, mince pies, brandy butter and great urns of tea were supplied. Once again, the guests tucked in with gusto. After tea, there were games and music and it seemed every type of entertainment had been laid on and many of the advisers came to join in the fun. Everywhere in the hall and adjoining rooms, something was happening. Around nine o'clock, Matt started up a conga. At first only five people got up to form a line and put their hands on the person in front's hips. The boys from the rock band got up and ten more people joined in. Aunt Maddie, Katya and Sharon, Charlie, Michael and even Arthur joined the line. In the end, almost half the guests were on their feet and the line circled the main hall, danced into the corridor, all singing '*Oh, the hokey-cokey!*' at the tops of their voices.

'This has been one of the top Christmases ever,' I said when it finished, and I collapsed onto a chair near Charlie. I couldn't have felt more surprised. A day I had been dreading had turned out to be better than I could have imagined. Porchester Park was so quiet, with everyone gone away and it had felt flat there despite the fabulous decorations. Here, it was buzzing with Christmas cheer – a group of people working together and a great atmosphere. I'd never felt the Christmas spirit more keenly, even though I knew it was bitter-sweet. It had been such a happy day but I felt so sad about the guests' situations. I only wished I could do more to help them, especially people like Arthur.

'I'm going to volunteer every year,' I said.

Charlie nodded. 'Me too. My band could come and play. I'm sure they'll all be up for it when I tell them. And then I am going to become very rich rock star so I can donate. I mean, *someone* has to pay for all of this and not just with their time.'

I glanced at Aunt Maddie who had sat down on a nearby chair. She had a big grin on her face. 'Well, your mum would certainly have enjoyed seeing you two wash up and peel vegetables!' she said. 'She'd be in hysterics over that.'

'Cheek!' I said.

She straightened her expression. 'Sorry. Couldn't help it. It's just great to have you two here and I'm so glad you enjoyed it. I think your mum would have loved it too.'

I nodded. It was *exactly* her kind of Christmas Day.

Sorted. Every year from now on, this is where I'd be. Somehow I could feel Mum smiling down on us – and not just because we'd done some washing up!

I'd found my perfect new Christmas tradition.

8
Riko

'So, you ready to rock with Riko?' asked Pia as we made our way over to the front of Porchester Park.

'Yeah,' I replied reluctantly. 'I guess she needs friends but I'm glad you're coming too.'

Last time I was up at the Mori's apartment, visiting the cats, Riko was moaning that Porchester Park was like a prison and how she was going crazy. While I was there, she asked her dad if she could go shopping with me now that we were friends. *Friends? That's new to me*, I'd thought but I'd agreed to show her round, especially when I heard she wanted to go to Harrods, as they had an awesome sale. Sure enough, she was waiting for us in reception with her father the first day the shops were open again after Christmas.

'I think I can trust you to look after my daughter, Jess,' said Mr Mori. 'You're a sensible girl. Stay together and you have my number if you need to call.'

'Da-*ad*,' said Riko as she bustled us out towards the waiting limo. 'I'll be fine. Come on, guys. Let's go.'

We got into the car and were soon being whisked away towards Harrods which was all of two minutes down the road. *Mad*, I thought.

Riko was in a good mood. '*Free-ee!*' she declared giving us a big smile and putting on her huge black sunglasses. 'I just want to merge with the crowds. No-one watching over me. No-one noticing me. I want to be invisible.'

I didn't say anything but the chances of her not being noticed were pretty unlikely dressed the way she was. She was wearing a vintage blue silk jacket, a massive pink scarf wound twice around her neck, denim shorts, sports sneakers and ripped fishnet tights. Her hair was piled on top of her head sticking out at all angles and kept in place with what looked like two red chopsticks. Like all her unusual outfits, it worked, but invisible she was not. I felt so boring next to her in my jeans and ordinary three-quarter-length red coat.

The car dropped us at the entrance to Harrods. The young American driver looked at his watch. 'I'll return in two hours,' he said. Riko didn't reply. She headed straight for the shop door.

'Thank you,' said Pia to the driver. 'We'll make sure we're here.'

Inside the shop, a doorman in a green-and-gold uniform glanced out at us, then opened the door. Immediately, we were swept into a frenzy of noisy, enthusiastic shoppers as they pushed and shoved their way down the aisles, eagerly looking for sales bargains. All around, I noticed different accents, – every country seemed to be represented here: Italian, Japanese, Indian, French, German, Arab, Americans – a united nation of bargain hunters under one roof.

'This place has got more pull for tourists than all the London museums and galleries put together,' I shouted to Pia above the babble.

'And it's much more fun,' said Riko as she forged her way forwards.

'Is there anything in particular you want?' Pia asked Riko when we caught up with her.

She shook her head and took her sunglasses off.

Her eyes shone with excitement. 'All of it!' she said and set off towards the cosmetics department.

We followed her with some difficulty as she darted this way and that through the throng of shoppers, only pausing occasionally to do serious damage to her dad's credit card. I looked at my watch and was amazed to see we'd been there for almost an hour. When Pia and I went shopping, we'd always take our time and have a good look around before buying anything. Riko was a whirlwind, grabbing a couple of designer purses here, scooping up a whole shelf-load of perfumes, lipsticks and eye shadows there, then moving on to scented candles. Once paid for, she'd toss the bags to us to carry for her, as if we were her servants.

'How about we go and get a drink?' I pleaded as another carrier bag was thrust my way. 'They do fab organic smoothies.'

Riko checked her watch then nodded. 'Um. Sure. Good idea. I'm just going to the Ladies then I'll join you.'

'Oh. I'd better come with you then,' I said.

Riko looked horrified. 'I'm not a baby.'

'I know but your dad said we had to be your minders and not leave you alone,' I said.

Riko rolled her eyes. 'Gimme a break, guys. We're just hanging out, OK? We've only got another hour before we're picked up. What are you? Prison warders? Come *on*. I'm a big girl, I can go to the bathroom by myself. Give me *some* respect.'

I glanced at Pia, who shrugged. 'Your life,' she said.

'OK,' I said, but I didn't feel happy about it. 'There's a café on the lower ground floor. Do you know where it is?'

Riko nodded. 'Sure. I *have* been here before you know. Down the escalator, right? Anyway, you have my mobile.' She didn't wait for an answer. She glanced quickly at her watch again, then took off.

'See you in five,' she called over her shoulder and then she was gone.

Pia glanced down at the bags piled all around us and laughed. 'You've got to admire her cheek. I wonder if she'd have helped us carry anything *we'd* bought.'

'Of course,' I said. 'NOT.'

We slowly picked our way through the crowd to the lower ground floor escalator but I couldn't resist the temptation to stop to try on a few perfumes.

'Mmm,' I said as we sniffed in tuberose, amber and vanilla scents.

Pia pulled me away. 'We'd better go,' she said. 'In case Lady Mori gets to the café before us.'

There was only a short queue of people waiting to be seated in the café. After a short while, a handsome man with a name tag that said Vincenzo showed us to an area in the corner of the café with white leather seats studded with silver buttons.

'Very posh and a half,' said Pia as Vincenzo gave her a large menu. She glanced at the drinks list. 'Oops. Poverty alert. A fresh juice costs seven pounds. Orange is five pounds. Um. Maybe we'd better skip drinks. I've only got a tenner and that has to last me the rest of the week.'

I took the menu from her and winced at the prices. 'We could share a bottle of pineapple juice, that'll only be three fifty.'

'Deal,' said Pia. 'You have the pine, I'll have the apple.'

Vincenzo came back to take our order and gave us a disapproving look when we asked for one drink between the two of us. He flounced off and a few minutes later, our drink arrived.

'I can't help but think about all the money being spent here,' I said, 'and how the people I met on Christmas Day had nothing.'

'I know but I'm sure a lot of these shoppers do their bit. I'm always reading about how rich people and celebrities do loads for charity. Some give away tons of dosh, others organise parties where everyone has to pay for their supper and then they auction stuff off,' said Pia as she took a slurp of the juice. 'Mm, yummy. And why *shouldn't* they enjoy their money too?'

'I guess. It's just a lot to get my head around. I seem to be experiencing amazing extremes lately, you know, the super rich and the seriously poor.'

Pia nodded. 'I know what you mean, but people do what they can in different ways. I mean, whose to say who does more good? Someone like your Aunt Maddie who gives her time or a millionaire who gives his money? Both make a difference.'

'I guess. But there's a huge imbalance in the world, don't you think?'

Pia laughed. 'You should become a politician if it bothers you so much. Me, I'd rather become very rich then make big donations to help out.'

'That's what Charlie says too. Hey, do you think

we should order something for Riko?' I took a tiny sip of our juice then handed the glass to Pia. She also took a small sip. We knew we had to make it last.

Pia pointed to a wall clock. 'She's been gone quite a while.'

'Bound to be a queue at the Ladies. Always is.'

'Or she's running up her credit card again.'

'Probably,' I said. 'You don't think she came while I was trying on perfume, do you? Maybe she was really quick, got here and didn't see us, then went to look for us.'

'Maybe but I doubt it. You stay here and I'll go and look then I'll text you when I find her.'

Pia went off and as I sat waiting, I saw Bridget O'Reilly waiting in the queue. She waved and came over. 'Hey, Jess. You all alone? Mind if join you?' Before I could answer, she'd tucked herself into Pia's empty seat. She tapped a foot against one of the heap of carrier bags by the chair. 'Any good bargains?'

'Some, there's a sale on.'

'That's why I'm here. Good Christmas?'

I nodded. 'Yes, actually.'

'What did you do?'

I glanced around, then took a sip of the juice. 'Oh,

you know, the usual.' I was determined not give anything away.

Bridget smiled. 'Not still worried about talking to me, are you?'

I shrugged a shoulder.

'Ah, who's to see us here? I've a few days' break left and I'm doing a bit of shopping and today, I'm not at all interested in where you live or who lives there. Now, would you like another juice?'

It was tempting but I shook my head. *No harm in a bit of a chat, though, as long as it's not about Porchester Park*, I thought. I liked Bridget and she was the only one of the paparazzi who didn't make me feel like I was a nobody. 'How was your Christmas, Bridget?'

'Oh, it was fine,' she said flatly.

'Did you go back to Ireland?'

Bridget shook her head. 'No. Both my parents have passed on now.'

'Any family over here?'

'Aren't you the inquisitive one today? Ever thought of becoming a journalist with that enquiring mind?'

'Sorry. I didn't mean to be nosy.'

Bridget smiled. 'That's OK. To be honest, Jess, Christmas isn't my favourite time of year. I do have family: a daughter, but she's off on her gap year. She's in Australia at the moment and, before you ask, I'm separated from my husband so I spent Christmas alone with the telly.' She made an attempt to laugh. 'Ah then, aren't I the sad one?' She sat up straight and smiled. 'Not really. It was fine.' I got the feeling she was acting brave and had actually been lonely over the holidays.

'I think it's a tough time for a lot of people,' I said. 'There's a lot of expectation and build up. I've been thinking about it a lot. We have to do an essay for school on the perfect holiday, that sort of thing.'

'A beach in the Caribbean with a cocktail in one hand and a good book in the other, now *that* would be my perfect holiday.'

'I think that's where a lot of the residents are,' I said then realised I'd let out private information and clamped my hand over my mouth. 'Oops!"

Bridget smiled. 'Ah go on, it's OK. I'm off-duty today so anything you say is off the record.'

Even though I liked Bridget, I wasn't totally convinced, so I decided to test her. A great idea flashed through my mind. I'd pretend to give her a really juicy story but it would be a monstrous fib. I'd tell her she wasn't to tell anyone then if it got mentioned in the paper, I'd know I couldn't trust her. If the story didn't appear, I'd know that I could.

'Actually there *is* something amazing happening.' Bridget leant forward. 'Tom Cruise is coming tomorrow and may be going to buy the penthouse duplex. Tomorrow morning in fact, at nine-thirty. All very hush hush.'

Bridget's eyes lit up. 'But I thought . . . is he really?'

I nodded. 'This is strictly between us, right? You said off-duty, off the record.'

'Of course,' said Bridget. 'You can trust me.'

At that moment, my phone bleeped that I had a text. It was Pia saying no sign of Riko. As I texted her to come back, Vincenzo came over to tell Bridget there was a table for her. I put my phone away.

'So. Tom Cruise, our secret, yeah?' I said. 'Dad would kill me if he knew I'd told you.'

Bridget stood up and nodded. 'Today I'm just another bargain hunter. Your secret's safe with me.' She put a finger to her lips, winked and walked away.

Well, we'll soon see about that, I thought, as I watched her take a table near the front of the café.

Moments later, Pia appeared. She looked flustered. 'Riko not been here, then?'

I shook my head and told her that I'd been

chatting with Bridget. She laughed when I told her about the Tom Cruise story. He'd been in town for a premiere, so it was plausible.

'Brilliant. We'll get all the gossip mags and check,' she said, then glanced at her watch. 'We should try calling Riko. I'm starting to get worried. She might have got lost. This place is vast.'

I pulled out the piece of paper with her number on and called it on my mobile.

'Bummer,' I said. 'It's gone to voicemail.'

Pia giggled. 'Maybe she's just on the loo.'

I shook my head. She had been gone a long time and I was beginning to feel anxious too. 'Maybe but . . . I think she got it into her head to lose us. She wanted a bit of time alone. Hell. Her dad's going to kill me if I go back without her. And so's my dad. Double death. What should we do?'

'Text her now. Tell her we're waiting in the café and to come right away. It'll be OK, Jess. She's probably trying on some clothes somewhere. You know how she said she longed for a bit of freedom. I can hardly blame her. She'll turn up soon.'

'I hope so.'

Five more minutes dragged by. Another five and still no sign of her. I was starting to get a bad feeling.

I got up and went over to Vincenzo. ''Scuse me. Are there any other cafés on this floor?'

'There are three down here. Over twenty in the whole shop,' he said and moved off to guide another customer to a vacant table.

I went back to Pia. 'More than twenty cafés! She could be at any one of them wondering where *we* are.'

'No. She'd have phoned,' said Pia. 'And we were clear that we were down here.'

'I guess. Oh God. The driver will be waiting out front for us in half an hour,' I said as I scanned the crowds.

'Plenty of time, then,' said Pia, but she didn't look as confident as she had earlier.

'You girls finished?' asked Vincenzo as he passed by again and took our empty glass. He indicated a waiting queue to the front of the café.

'Oh yes. Sorry. Thank you. Um, please could you tell me where the nearest Ladies is?' I asked.

'First floor is the closest,' said Vincenzo and he indicated up as if to say, up on other floors. 'All signposted.'

We got up, paid our bill then walked outside the café. I noticed that there were a bunch of store guides on a table to the left. I took one. Each floor looked like a maze with stairs, escalators, cloakrooms and halls. My unease was making my stomach churn. Seven vast floors and thousands of people. We were never going to find her. I tried to call her but again, it went to voicemail. I sent a text saying that we were on the lower floor. I cursed myself for letting her out of my sight.

'Should we stay here in case she comes to find us or go and look for her?' asked Pia.

'God, I don't know. She didn't say which cloakroom she was going to or on which floor. And Vincenzo said there are loads of cafés. She could be anywhere. Arghhhh. If we go looking for her, she may come down here and wonder where we are. Oh, I could kill the spoilt brat. I *wish* she'd answer her phone.'

'OK. Decision time. You stay here. I'll go and look again,' said Pia. 'Call me if she appears and I'll call you if I find her.'

'Good plan,' I said. 'Except probably better if *you* stay and *I* go and look. I'm taller and can see over more heads.'

Pia stood on her tiptoes and looked out at the crowd. 'Hmm. Guess you might be right. You sure she has your number?'

I nodded. 'Yes. If she's lost, she could call me. I blooming well wish she would.'

Pia looked at her watch. 'Stay calm, Sergeant Hall. Synchronise watches, now start mission.'

I saluted her. 'And don't move from this spot. I don't want to lose you too.'

Pia returned my salute then I raced up the closest escalators to the ground floor then took another going up. Even though I felt really anxious, I couldn't help noticing how stunning it was as I floated up through what seemed like a real underground Egyptian temple. All the walls were painted deep gold with hieroglyphics. Here and there, massive statues silently watched the manic shoppers. *No wonder all these tourists are here*, I thought as I scanned the crowds going up and down. *It's like being in a* real *temple, only with loads of fab stuff on sale*. I got off at the first floor and pushed my way to the nearest Ladies. A notice on the door said, **CLOSED. Apologies. Try Second Floor.** *Oh NO*, I thought as I raced off back to the escalator. Inside I was freaking out as I imagined how Dad was going to react when he found out I'd lost Riko.

After a frantic search, I eventually found the second floor Ladies.

'Medical emergency,' I called and ran past a dozen or so women standing in line. All the cubicles were occupied.

'Riko, are you in there?' I called.

An elderly lady stepped out of one of the cubicles a few moments later and gave me a peculiar look.

'Um, just looking for my friend,' I said and dashed out past the ladies in the queue again, as they looked daggers at me. I glanced up and down the corridor for the escalator sign. I saw one and followed the directions to where I could see escalators to all floors. But they weren't the ones I'd been on previously. *God. Where am I?* I wondered as I hopped on. *It's so easy to get lost in this place.* I pulled out my guide to see how many escalators there were. *Dozens. Riko might be lost but now so am I*, I thought as panic hit me again.

I hopped on the ascending escalator, scanned the crowds again and thought I glimpsed Riko on the descending escalator opposite. Was it her? I couldn't be sure. I didn't have a clear view as there were so many people packed onto it. I could only see the back of the girl's head but she had a blue jacket on and I thought I glimpsed a flash of red in her hair. Chopsticks. It *must* be her. She appeared to be with someone. A guy. Again, I could only see the back of him and couldn't be sure if she was actually with him or just happened to standing next to him on the escalator. I strained to get a better look just as an enormous Indian man carrying a huge packet pushed past me, further obscuring my view. When I could see again, the girl had disappeared, swallowed up into the endlessly moving wave of shoppers. But I wasn't going to lose her. I ran up the rest of my escalator, hopped onto the descending one, ran down the left hand side and back onto the second floor. I raced around the floor through kitchenware, bed-linens, china, luggage. But no sign of Riko. *And she wouldn't be looking at this stuff anyway*, I decided.

I called Pia. 'Any luck?'

'She's not down here. Five minutes to go until the driver's here to collect us.'

The knot in my stomach tightened, making it hard to breathe. I would be grounded for the rest of eternity. My life was over.

I was feeling utterly miserable when a hand suddenly slapped on my shoulder. I almost jumped out of my skin. 'There you are,' said a familiar voice.

I turned. It was Riko.

'Here *I* am? Where've *you* been?'

Riko grinned. 'Hey. Don't sweat it. I haven't been anywhere.'

'But you were supposed to meet us in the café.'

She grinned. 'Sorr*ee*. I'm always losing track of time. But it's cool, yeah?' She didn't look sorry at all as she glanced at her watch and waggled her wrist at me. 'We're still on time, yeah?'

'Yes, so that's all right then. I'll let Pia know we're ready to go,' I said sharply. I felt cross with her for getting us so worried. I texted Pia to meet us at the entrance then went back to Riko, who was now checking out the bath gels in the bathshop. She appeared totally unconcerned about the scare. 'Yes, we're on time, Riko, but you gave us a fright. Your dad and mine would have been furious if they'd known we'd split up.'

Riko gave me a fake smile. 'Hey chill, Jess. I'm here now, so what's the problem?' She linked arms with me. 'Don't be mad with me, Jess Hall. I won't get lost again. Promise. And, anyway, dads are always cross, right?'

'Why did you turn your phone off?' I asked. I was still annoyed with her.

'Did I?' She pulled it out from her pocket. 'Um . . . it's new. Sometimes I er . . . hit the silent button and don't realise. Silly me. But hey, Jessie, I wouldn't have dropped you in it, really I wouldn't. You're my good friend.'

Yeah right, I thought as we took the escalators down. *Friends don't wander off and not say where they're going, Riko. And don't call me Jessie!*

'I can't tell you how fabulous freedom is, if only for a short while,' continued Riko. 'To be on my own with no-one watching my every move.'

'I guess I can understand that,' I said begrudgingly as we reached the ground floor where Pia spotted us and came to join us.

'Where the hell were you, Riko?' she demanded. Pia was never one to mince her words. 'Jess and I were freaking out. What if you'd been kidnapped or something had happened to you? *We'd* have been right in it, that's what. Or don't you ever think of other people?' She shoved Riko's bags at her. 'And I'm not carrying these any more either. I believe they belong to you.'

Riko looked taken aback by Pia's outburst but it made me want to giggle. She was voicing exactly what I had been too polite to say. Riko looked at a loss as to what to do for a few moments then she reached into one of the carrier bags and pulled out two small boxes. She gave one to me and one to Pia.

'I'm sorry. Truly I am. And see, I got you a scented candle each to say thank you for today. For being my friends and not my minders. Yes? Understand? The candles are amber and fig. Mm. Smell fab.'

I felt like I was being paid off. Pia clearly felt the same.

'Thanks, Riko, but we don't need presents to be your friend. Just don't go wandering off again, right?' she said. 'And you're right. We're not your minders but your dad *is* holding us responsible for showing you around.'

'Please take the candles all the same,' she said. 'I realise now that I worried you.' She attempted to look apologetic but part of me felt like I couldn't trust her and that she was putting on an act. However, as she continued to press the candles at us, we eventually accepted them.

'Thanks, Riko,' I said.

She was all smiles now and linked arms with Pia and me as we went out to the car. 'Good. Now we're all friends again. I'm very happy to have had this time with you,' she said.

I wasn't though. The all-pals-together act felt false to me. She had a secret and friends shared secrets. No way was she sharing hers with me.

9
Boy talk

'Yay,' I said as I glanced at my computer the next morning. 'A message from Tom! He and Josh have been on the facebook site and left some tips for us about boys.'

'No way,' said Pia. 'Let's have a look.' She squeezed next to me on my chair and peered at the screen.

'And look, a party invite at last!' I said. 'He says, "Hey Hall, been missing your particular brand of madness. Party at my place New Year's Eve. Bring your strange midget friend." Do you think he means you?'

'Probably. Blooming cheek. He can stuff his invite. I mean, you're not going to go are you? Not after the way he's treated you?'

'There'll be other boys there. I will go, but I'll ignore him. I'll get off with another boy or maybe even a few boys and show him that I've moved on and don't care.'

Pia raised an eyebrow. 'Yeah, right,' she said. 'I can see that.'

'But a party . . . It would be fun.'

Pia frowned. 'I don't want to see you get hurt.'

'I'll risk it. It's been so boring. Chaperoning Riko. Being Miss Goody-two-shoes on Christmas Day with Aunt Maddie, even though I did enjoy it in the end. It'll be so nice to hang out with some people our own age from school and not think about stuff like who's rich, who's poor, how to save the world, end poverty and bring peace on Earth and all before my sixteenth birthday. It's all right for you, you're all loved up at the moment.' She was too. I'd tried not to mind but it was hard having a best mate with a boyfriend who wasn't as available as usual. Whenever I called she was over at Henry's listening to music or he was at hers watching a DVD. I felt like a great, goosing gooseberry and although Pia always invited me along to whatever they were doing, it felt like another case of them and me. The rich and me. The homeless and me. Henry, Pia and me. Charlie, Tom and me. Mainly *me* out of a limb on my own with a million mixed feelings. I was getting fed up of it and I wanted to have a night having a laugh with nothing more serious to think about than pulling boys – although actually that was *very* serious.

'So. What nuggets of wisdom have they sent us?' asked Pia as she scrolled down to see what they'd written. I began to read. '"You don't need to try too hard. Most of us are grateful for any attention from a girl." Ah, Josh would have written that. It's true. His only criteria for a girl is that she's breathing.'

'"If you like a boy, TELL HIM,"' I read. '"We are not mind-readers and never will be. We need all the guidance and help we can get. We are useless when it comes to reading girls. Think of us as emotionally dyslexic and you won't go far wrong. Most of us don't recognise flirting even when it's coming right at us." Hmm. Doubt Tom wrote that so I reckon that's one from Josh again.'

'"We will never be slushy with you in front of our

mates,"' read Pia. '"We might be nuts about you but it's not cool to show it." Hmm. I think Tom might be trying to tell you something.'

'No way. He's the King of Confidence,' I said and read on. '"Try to understand that a boy wants to be with you but simultaneously wants to be left alone. Us boys can be contradictory and complicated too, but mainly we're just simple." That doesn't sound like Josh, does it? Maybe Tom *is* trying to tell me something.'

Pia read the next line from the screen. '"Boys are very anxious about rejection. Be kind to us. We have feelings too."'

'Definitely Josh again!' we chorused.

'Tom's probably never been rejected,' I added.

'"Boys are intimidated by beautiful girls,"' read Pia.

'Josh again,' I said. Pia nodded in agreement.

'"Be kind when dumping us, treat people as you expect to be treated yourself,"' I continued. 'That's a good point.'

'"Don't try and change us. We don't like it,"' Pia read out. 'Tom?'

I nodded. 'Yeah. Charlie says that too. He says he hates it when girls start telling him how to dress or wear his hair. Big no no.'

'"Have fun in a relationship before you get serious,"' read Pia. 'I think deffo Tom is trying to tell you something.'

'That's decided, then,' I said. 'I will go to his party and I will have fun.'

'Will come to party and bring strange midget friend,' I typed quickly then pressed reply before Pia could object. 'There. Done. I'm sure you can bring Henry now that you're joined at the hip.'

Pia gave me a salute. 'Yes, SIR – and as for being joined at the hip, for that, you're coming to the movies with me and Henry this afternoon and I won't take no for an answer.'

I saluted her back. 'Yes, SIR.'

As we were getting ready, my phone rang. It was Riko.

'Jess, what are you doing this afternoon?' She sounded agitated.

'Apparently going to the movies with Sergeant Major Pia,' I said. I was glad I had something to do in case Riko wanted to hang out.

'Cool. What time are you going?'

'In about half an hour.'

'Where?'

'A cinema down the King's Road.'

'Great. OK. I'll meet you in reception. I can get my dad's chauffeur to drive us.'

'I . . . er—' It was too late to object. She'd gone.

I put down the phone.

'What was all that about?' asked Pia.

'I think we've just been outdone in the Sergeant Major stakes,' I said. 'That girl is a master!'

Riko was waiting for us in reception and once again, we were driven in her dad's limo. Luckily this time, the journey was further so I could enjoy the ride. *I could really get used to this*, I thought as the car purred along the road and I stared out at all the pedestrians, buttoned up against the dull, cold day. Riko wasn't saying much. She still seemed agitated and kept looking at her watch. I felt uncomfortable about the whole deal. It was as if she was controlling my life and I didn't like it. Pia and Henry sat holding hands, seemingly oblivious to it all. *In their love bubble*, I thought. They were even wearing matching red scarves and red Converse sneakers.

'How's the survey going, Jess?' Henry asked.

I didn't feel much like talking so I shrugged a shoulder.

'It's about what boys want, isn't it?' he asked.

'And what girls want too,' said Pia.

Henry laughed. 'Ask a girl what she wants and you'll get lectured for days.' He rolled his eyes. 'Communication. Growing as a couple. Respect.'

Pia slapped his arm. 'Hey mister, I'm not like that. So come on, then, tell us. What *do* boys want?'

Henry grinned. 'Come naked. Bring beer.'

This time, it was mine and Pia's turn to roll our eyes. Riko didn't appear to be listening. She was busy texting someone and when I glanced down I was sure she'd written the road we were going to as if she was giving someone directions. When she saw me looking, she turned away so I couldn't see.

'You OK?' I asked, after the driver had let us out of the car and we went to join the line to get our tickets.

'Yeah, I'm good,' she said unenthusiastically as she got out her phone again and checked for texts. It appeared that there was one and she turned away to read it and reply.

What's with all the secrecy? I wondered.

'What's up?' I asked when she turned back to me then quickly put her phone away.

'Oh, you know,' she said. 'Same ole. My dad. He won't get off my case. I'm sixteen, no longer a kid but that's how he treats me.' We got our tickets then Riko waved hers to the driver who was now hovering a short distance away. 'We'll be fine now,' she called to him. 'See you here after the movie.'

The driver nodded and got back in his car. I noticed a couple of girls from our school going in to see the film with their boyfriends. Even though Riko was weird, part of me was glad she'd come along because at least I didn't look like the only sad singleton.

'Yeah, dads,' I said. 'Tell me about it.' I was trying to sympathise but actually my dad had been pretty cool with me lately. In fact, he probably gave me too much freedom. He never knew where I was half the time. He was too busy running the apartment block.

'No,' she said. 'It's different for you. *You* can come and go as you please. I have no freedom at all. In fact, it's a miracle my parents have let me out with you.'

'You're not going to go missing like that day in Harrods, are you?'

Riko looked sheepish. 'No way. Anyhow, I didn't go missing. Not really. I hate this time of year. I can't wait for it to be over. I miss my mates from school. I don't know anyone in London. I . . . Oh, I didn't mean to be rude. Of course I know you and Pia, but . . .'

She didn't have to say it. I wasn't from her world and she was right. My life was different. I went to school and came home at night. Riko went to boarding school and only saw her family in the holidays. My best mate lived next door. Meg and Flo weren't far away. 'It must be hard for you,' I said. 'I mean, how do you get to meet people? How do you get to meet *boys*?'

'Exactly.' She nodded and looked sad. 'People think we have it all but actually I can't see who I want to. I mean . . . I'm lonely in the holidays.'

Alisha had said something similar to me when we'd first got to know each other – that with the lifestyle they had, it was sometimes like living in a gilded cage.

'What would be your perfect holiday, then?' I asked.

Riko smiled for the first time that day. 'Perfect? Hmm . . . Somewhere romantic, I think. Paris with a boy I really liked – in the snow. No minders. No Mum and Dad asking, where are you going? What are you doing? Who are you talking to? Just being able to go where I want, when I want. Just for a short time. Heaven.'

'Most people want to spend the holidays with their family,' I said.

'Yeah. Some of it. Not *all* of it. My parents are so strict.'

As we went into the cinema, I spotted the boy I'd seen a few weeks ago outside the apartment block. He was looking our way. I nudged Riko.

'I don't want to worry you but I think we may be being followed,' I said.

Riko whipped her head round to look but the boy moved away. 'By who? Where?'

'He's gone. A boy I've seen hanging about outside Porchester Park. I think he saw me look at him.'

Riko was straining to see. 'What did he look like?'

'Slim. Dark. Nice-looking. I thought he was one of the paparazzi at first but he could be a stalker.'

Riko burst out laughing as she scrutinised the crowds. 'Kidnapper alert!' she said and it felt as if she was teasing me.

'Hey. It does happen sometimes. Do you think we should tell your dad?'

Riko's expression changed. 'NO! God no. Can you imagine? That would be the end of all my trips out with you. Please don't say anything, Jess. We aren't being followed. I was joking about a stalker. It was probably a coincidence that you saw him here.'

'Are you sure? Because I kind of feel responsible for you.'

'Chill. I'm fine. Dad knows where we are. Our driver's waiting outside. Let's go in and enjoy the movie but . . . first I need to use the Ladies.'

Pia glanced at me. 'Me too,' she said.

Riko looked annoyed. 'Hey come on, I've told you before, I don't need a chaperone.'

'I know,' said Pia. 'But I need to use the Ladies too and quite honestly, after last time, we're not risking losing you again.'

Riko's face looked like thunder as Pia escorted her off. Over her shoulder, Pia turned and winked.

When they returned and we took our seats, I could see that Riko was fuming. *What's her problem?* I wondered. *She seemed almost happy to think that she might have a stalker.* Mr Mori had put her in my care and I liked him and didn't want to let him down. I needed to ask someone at Porchester Park if they'd seen anyone hanging about in case Riko was in any kind of danger. *She* might not take it seriously but *I* did. But I couldn't ask Yoram or Didier. It would get straight back to Dad. *Bridget!* I thought. *We're kind of friends now and she's always outside the apartment block.* Plus it appeared that Bridget had kept her promise and was trustworthy after all. There hadn't been a whisper about Tom Cruise in the press after my test for her. Pia and I had checked in all the papers that were delivered to reception every day and he hadn't got a mention in any of them.

As the movie credits started up, I noticed that Riko had got her phone out and typed a text. The phone bleeped back seconds later.

'School mate?' I whispered.

'Sort of,' she replied with a slight shift of her shoulder away from me as if to say, 'It's private.'

'Shh,' said a lady behind us. 'The movie's about to start.'

I settled back into my seat but, next to me, I could feel that Riko was restless. She kept turning round as if she was looking for someone. Maybe she was looking for the boy. Maybe she was so lonely, she was desperate for any attention, even from a stalker. Whatever the story, there was *something* going on in the life of Riko Mori that she wasn't letting on about, that was for sure.

10
New friend

'Bridget, can I talk to you a sec?' I asked when I found her the next day. She was having a coffee in the café opposite Porchester Park.

She indicated the empty seat next to her. 'Sure. How can I help?'

I sat down and glanced out of the window towards Porchester Park to make sure that Yoram or Didier weren't watching. I could see Didier at a car that had drawn up, so I was safe. 'Um. Well, I wanted to ask, have you seen anyone strange hanging about round here?'

Bridget laughed. 'Ah, you mean apart from that

bunch of no-hopers over there?' she asked as she indicated the usual gathered crowd of paparazzi outside. There were fewer of them today I noticed, only four, and they were chatting amongst themselves.

'No. Not them. I wondered if you'd seen anyone who appears to be maybe watching the place?'

'Sounds intriguing, Jess. Do you mean old Eddie there?' she asked and looked in the direction of the homeless man who had taken up residence in a shop doorway again.

'No. Not him. Younger. Maybe late teens, early twenties?'

'Ah now, is this an admirer you have?'

'No. Not me. Just I thought I'd seen someone hanging around watching Porchester Park.'

Bridget thought for a few moments. 'Hard to say. With the paparazzi permanently parked outside, people often stop and stare – probably hoping to get a glimpse of someone famous. They're only tourists, passers-by. They soon move on when there's nothing to see but . . . come to think of it, there has been a boy on a few occasions. I took no notice the first few times but he does seem to be here quite frequently. Never stays long though. Why do you ask?'

'Oh, nothing.'

'Sure,' said Bridget. 'Nothing that hides a thousand secrets. Is he a boyfriend of yours?'

'Mine? No! Just . . . I've seen someone around a few times and I've read stories about rich people being stalked or kidnapped.'

'My but you have an active imagination. We'll have to call you Agent Jess. I wouldn't worry though. I doubt anyone would get past your men over there.' Bridget glanced towards the front of Porchester Park where Didier had now taken up his usual position outside. 'Plus the security inside is tight, isn't it?'

'Designed by the SAS,' I said then clapped my hand over my mouth. 'Oops. I wasn't supposed to tell you that. Please don't write it.'

'In case the SAS track you down,' said Bridget with a laugh. 'Don't worry. Your secret's safe with me. Tell you what. I'll keep an eye out and let you know if he comes back again. Anyway, how's yourself, Jess?'

'OK. Kind of looking forward to getting back to school if I'm honest.'

'No! What teen your age ever says that?'

'My mates have been away and Porchester Park is empty.'

Bridget nodded. 'I know. I might be moving on myself soon and as you've probably noticed, our numbers are down. There was a rumour Tom Cruise was coming to town but he never showed.' She had a twinkle in her eye when she said it and I got the feeling that she knew that I'd told her a lie.

'Er. No, he didn't, did he?' I said sheepishly.

'Can *you* keep a secret?'

I nodded. 'There was talk that George Clooney was taking an apartment here. No-one knows for sure but that's why a few of us are hanging around today, even though it's New Year's Eve. He's definitely in town.'

'I haven't heard Dad mention it,' I said. 'Not that he talks to me about who's buying into the place.'

'Age-old story,' said Bridget.

I laughed. 'My dad's OK,' I said.

Bridget glanced out of the café window at Porchester Park. 'It's quite a rare situation you live in over there,' she said.

'I guess.'

'Different worlds, hey?'

'Yeah.'

Bridget turned back to look at me. 'Must be hard for you in some ways, living a stone's throw away from people who have everything and being on the outside. That's how *I* feel some days, anyway. Seeing them roll up in their limos. Having it all. Us and them.'

I felt as if she'd hit a nerve. That was exactly how it felt some days, but though I was warming to Bridget, I didn't like her putting me in the same boat as her.

'I'm not exactly on the outside,' I said.

'Are you not? And how's that?'

'I . . .' I wanted her to know that, actually, I was accepted by some of the rich residents. That I *was* in with the in-crowd, unlike her who really *was* an outsider.

'Some of them are my mates.'

'Are they now?'

'Oh yes. Like I'm good friends with Alisha Lewis.'

Bridget looked impressed. 'Jefferson Lewis's daughter?'

I nodded. 'She's away. She'll be back soon.'

'And I've seen you go out with the Japanese girl? Isn't she Mr Mori's daughter?'

I couldn't help it – it felt good showing off that I knew some of them personally. 'Riko. Yeah. I've been out with her a few times but Alisha's more my friend.'

'That's nice. Good to have friends.'

I nodded. 'Yeah.'

'And what are they like?'

I hesitated then remembered the agreement that Jefferson Lewis had with the press – that they could photograph him but had to leave his children alone. It was surely safe to talk about them, especially to Bridget. 'Alisha's cool. Riko's harder to get to know, like some days she's more open that others. Sometimes I think it's hard for people my age at Porchester Park. Some of them I haven't even seen, they live in such an exclusive world. Although it's probably fab on many levels, I'd hate it. It's like there's a wall between them and the rest of the world.'

Bridget nodded. 'I think you're right, Jess. A gilded cage.'

'That's exactly what I said. Like, Riko's at boarding school and finds it hard in the holidays. She told me how lonely she gets.'

'Is that so? Understandable,' said Bridget. 'I've often thought that. These rich teens don't get the freedom you girls get. I mean, how are they supposed to get out and meet boys for one thing?'

'Exactly,' I said. It seemed like Bridget really understood and it was good to talk to someone who seemed genuinely interested. If I tried to talk to Dad about the teen residents, he always seemed to make out that it was none of my business. 'When I first moved in, I thought they had it all but when I got to know Alisha, I realised that she just wanted what I had. Mad that, isn't it? Like, she enjoys being rich and stuff but she knows that mates are what's important.'

'They are, especially at your age. You need people you can trust. That must be another problem for them. They don't know who wants to be friends with them genuinely or who wants to get in with them because of who their parents are in the hope that a bit of the glitter will rub off.'

'Yeah. I never thought about that until I got to know Alisha and then Riko. Riko can't wait to get back to school – to be back with her friends. She wants to go out and explore London but if she does, she has to have a minder or a driver with her. She was telling me how much she hates it.' Suddenly I felt I'd said too much. Not that I'd dropped any state secrets but I'd said more than usual. 'Er . . . better go, Bridget.'

'Nice talking to you, Jess. You take of yourself now,' said Bridget and she went back to her coffee. 'And I am sure those girls are lucky to have a friend like you.

Will you be doing something nice then, this evening?'

I nodded. 'Party.'

'Lucky old you.'

'Thanks. Um, OK, bye,' I said.

'And I'll look out for that boy,' she called as I got up and went towards the door. *I like Bridget*, I thought as I left. *She seems like a nice woman. Maybe one day I'll even bring her out a cup of coffee*.

As I went past Eddie, I dropped a few coins in the hat he always had out in front of him. Since Christmas Day, I always dropped something in. He never acknowledged the money I left or me, but that was OK. I knew that he would have a story about how he came to be homeless and he was maybe proud. Why should he thank everyone?

'Come in, totty,' said Josh as he opened the door at Tom's house that evening.

I pushed past him. 'Get a life, saddo.'

'You know you want me, Hall,' he said.

'In your dreams, Nash.'

Josh grinned and shut the door. 'Your mates are already here in the kitchen,' he said.

I pushed my way through the wall-to-wall teens

crammed in the corridor and headed towards the back. Anyone trying to have a conversation had to shout to make themselves heard over the loud music that pounded out of a room to the right. There were a few faces I recognised but no sign of Tom as I made my way to the kitchen. I was wearing a black dress that Pia's mum had lent me. It was part of the new sophisticated me. If Tom liked a challenge, I'd give him one. I was going to be cool, grown up and knock the socks off him with my new look and swept up hair à la Blair Waldorf in *Gossip Girl*. He would swoon at my feet. I would step over him and ignore him for most of the party by which time he would be so frustrated he'd be gagging for me. Only then would I snog him, just as the clock chimed midnight. Plan A. Sorted.

'Hey, Jess,' called Meg.

I turned and saw my crowd hovering around the drinks counter. Pia, Henry, Flo and Meg.

'Yay,' I said. 'The gang are back together. I've missed you guys sooooo much.'

Flo and Meg gave me a big hug and, not to be left out, Pia came to join in.

'Lesbos,' said Josh as he came up behind me.

'You're just jealous,' I said.

'Well *I* certainly am,' said a familiar voice.

I turned and there he was, looking as heart-stoppingly gorgeous as always in black jeans and a black T-shirt. Tom. I told myself to close my mouth, breathe and be coo-el.

'Oh hellar. Hor are ye-ou?' I said in a voice that was supposed to sound sophisticated but came out like I was being throttled.

'You had a voice transplant over the holidays?' asked Tom.

'Christmas present from the Queen,' I said. 'It's a rare and expensive voice elixir. Came in a bottle. Two drops a day and you talk posh.' *Shut up, shut up now, what are you saying? NOT cool, not cool*, I thought. Even Pia was looking at me as if I was mad. I glanced over at her and shrugged to let her know I had no idea what I was doing either.

'Great idea,' said Tom. 'I like that. Imagine. You could have all sorts of flavours that give all sorts of accents. Yeah, Hall. Interesting concept. I like that.'

'You d . . . do?' I stuttered. 'I mean, yeah. Interesting concept. I'm full of them.'

'I like girls who think outside the box,' said Tom.

'What box?' I blurted and Tom laughed. I laughed with him though I had no idea why. *Outside the box? What was he on about?*

'You do make me laugh, Hall,' he said.

NOT my plan. I didn't want to make him laugh. I wanted to make him slaver with desire. I wanted him to feel some of the ache I'd felt in wanting him but him not appearing to feel the same way. 'Um. How was your Christmas?' I asked then cursed myself for saying something so mundane.

He came and put his arm around me. 'I was lonely without you,' he said.

Oh, that's good, I thought and tried not to show that my knees had just gone weak.

Josh put two fingers in his mouth. 'Yeugh. Slush alert,' he said.

Tom pulled me out into the hall away from the others. 'So how's the survey going?' he asked. 'You a boy expert now?'

'Always was,' I said. *Liar, liar pants on fire*, I thought. 'Ah oui. Absolutement.' *And now I've gone French! Pourquoi? Pourquoi? My brain must be going into meltdown*.

'OK. So what am I thinking now?' he asked and he leant forward.

'Um . . .' My brain froze as he put his hand under my chin and tilted it up towards him. 'You're thinking about . . . OH MY GOD!'

Tom leapt back as a red-headed boy lurched forward to the left of us and threw up all over the wall. His puke stank of boiled alcohol.

'Ewwww,' I said as he staggered off, with Tom chasing after him, cursing at his back. *So much for our romantic moment*, I thought as I turned back to find my mates. *Snogsville just turned into Puketown*.

For the rest of the party, I hardly saw Tom apart from him rushing around with a bucket and large bottle of disinfectant. I tried flirting with a few boys but my heart wasn't really in it. I only had eyes for Tom and he only had time to clean up before his parents got back.

When the clock chimed midnight, I watched as Henry snogged Pia, Meg snogged Josh, Flo even got Charlie, although it looked as though she had him in an arm-lock. I stood alone and watched Tom, his face like thunder, as he marched the redheaded puker over to the front door and threw him out. *Plan A. Not sorted. Happy New Year to me*, I thought. *On my own again. Bummer.*

11
Exclusive!

'Ohmigod,' said Pia on the other end of the phone. 'Have you seen it?'

'How could I miss it?' I said. 'It's all over the third page of the paper. Dad hit the roof. I've never seen him like this.' He'd stormed in around eight that morning with a newspaper in his hand and a vein pulsing angrily on his forehead. He was ranting about a leak in the building. At first I thought he was talking about the plumbing, then he slammed the paper down in front of me and Charlie. There it was. **Exclusive by Bridget O'Reilly. Super-Rich Kids Not So Super?** was the heading. **Lonely teens at the top** was the line underneath. She'd written a piece about rich teenagers with quotes from a close anonymous source. Word for word what *I'd* said to her. I felt a sick feeling in the pit of my stomach as I read it.

'"They live in an exclusive world but there's a wall between them and the rest of the world. A gilded cage," my source told me. "I thought they had it all but mates are what's important and how are they supposed to meet people, especially boys? Girls like Riko Mori, daughter of entrepreneur, Yoshiki Mori, find it hard in the holidays. She gets lonely," said my source. "She can't wait to get back to school. She wants to explore London but can't without a minder."'

The words 'my source' seemed to scream out at me as if they were written in red capitals. As if they spelt out JESS HALL. TRAITOR. And all because I had wanted to prove to Bridget that I wasn't like her. I wasn't an outsider, I was in with the in-crowd. *This day can't get any worse*, I'd thought as I'd glanced at Dad. He looked as freaked out as I was.

'But where do you think she got details like that?' asked Pia. 'Sounds to me like she spoke to a member of staff or someone who really knew the families. It has to be someone who works at Porchester Park – a driver or a maid. Could be anyone.'

'Yes but it wasn't. It was *me*, Pia. *I* spoke to her on New Year's Eve. She certainly didn't waste any time – it's only January the second now.'

'You!' Pia exclaimed. She was silent for a few moments while she took it in. 'Shit.'

'I know. Double.'

'But you *knew* not to talk to her.'

'Oh P, don't have a go at me. I feel bad enough as it is. Don't you think I've cursed myself and my stupidity a thousand times already this morning? I thought . . . I thought Bridget was my friend. I *thought* I could trust her.'

'Some friend, but that's what some journalists do. They pal up with you, get you to feel like you're in their confidence so you spill the beans. It's part of the job.'

'I know. I *knew* that. Dad's hammered it home enough times. I can't believe I fell for it. I could kick myself.'

'You haven't told him it was you, have you?'

'No way. He'd kill me. But . . . what do I do?'

'Oh God, I don't know. Leave home. Get a throat infection and lose your voice. Hide under the bed for a day or two. Keep out of your dad's way, that's for certain, as knowing you, you'll blurt something out and give the game away.'

'I know. He'd be so mad if he found out it was me, plus how would it reflect on *him*? I mean, after all the times he's warned me – not just about not talking to them but also about how my behaviour reflects back on him as general manager.'

'Does he suspect you?'

'Don't think so. He thinks it was one of the staff.'

'So keep it zipped, that's what I'd do.'

'And you, Pia. Please don't tell Henry or he might tell his dad and he'll tell mine.'

'We're mates,' said Pia. 'I won't say a word.'

'Nor to Meg or Flo either, or Charlie.'

'Hey, chill. Listen, Jess, it'll blow over. It will. When there's a story like this in the paper, my mum always says, today's news, tomorrow's fish-and-chip paper. Lie low and wait until the storm is over.'

'Good plan,' I said but after I'd put down the phone, I still felt mortified. What would Riko think when she saw it? And Alisha? Both were mentioned by name. Someone was bound to blab about it to Alisha. Would she know it was me? Of course she would. She was a smart cookie and was bound to work it out and that would be the end of our friendship, not to mention what JJ would think of me.

For the next half hour, I tried telling myself that it would all blow over. Pia's mum was right, the story would soon be yesterday's news. I tried to busy myself with facebook but even the last messages posted weren't enough to make me forget what I'd done.

A girl called Lisbeth had written that her top tip was to manufacture times to spend with boys when they didn't feel threatened – like a group outing or a mutual project which gave time to hang out and get to know someone without them feeling that they were on a date. 'Boys are more relaxed at times like this,' she said.

Who cares about pulling boys when friendships with girls are at stake? I thought. *I am dooooooomed. If only I could turn the clock back a week. If only I hadn't trusted that rat Bridget. If only I'd been smarter. If only, if only, if only . . .*

'Jess. Get down here *right* now,' called Dad from downstairs.

I dashed down, my heart thumping in my chest. He'd found out it was me. I knew it. *How should I be? Apologetic? Crying? Begging forgiveness? Oh God, I hate this. I hate myself.*

I decided that I'd let him come out with it first. 'What is it?' I asked.

'Riko Mori. She's disappeared.'

'Riko! *Disappeared?* No! When?' My heart began to beat even faster as a panic hit me.

'This morning.'

'Where to?'

'That's what we're trying to find out,' said Dad. 'You've spent a little time with her lately. Have you any idea where she might have gone? Any clue? Now *think*, Jess, think. This is really important.'

'No,' I said. 'I've no idea where she might go. I don't know.' *This is my fault*, I thought. *She's seen the article and done a runner*. 'I . . . she was always talking about not liking being out with a minder.'

'So where do you think she might have gone?'

'Er . . . shopping? Maybe she just wanted some time on her own.'

'Maybe,' said Dad. 'But *where*, Jess? If anything comes to mind let me know immediately, won't you? In the meantime, we just have to pray that she shows up. Especially after that article. Mr Mori is livid, and now this.' I felt doubly bad because he looked so worried and that was my fault too. My stomach felt as if I'd swallowed a ton of bricks and I thought I was going to be sick. At that moment, Dad's phone rang. The vein on his forehead began pulsing again as he took the call – that always signalled bad news.

'What is it?' I said.

Dad sighed heavily. 'Riko's passport is missing. That means she could have gone anywhere.' He sat down on the sofa and held his head in his hands.

I'd thought today couldn't get any worse. I was wrong. It just had and it wasn't even midday yet.

12
Confession

Another hour went by and still no news of Riko. By early afternoon, I was in a terrible state. I couldn't eat, couldn't drink, couldn't think straight. I could hardly breathe. Dad had gone to meet the police to fill them in on what he knew. Pia had gone out shopping in the sales with her mum but she kept sending me texts saying: 'It'll be OK.' 'Call if you need to.' 'Everything passes.'

I knew she meant well but her messages weren't helping. I desperately needed someone to talk to. I glanced over at the photo of my mum. *I wish you were here*, I thought. *You'd know what to do*. *What to say*. I turned to Dave, who was sitting on the end of my bed. 'I need help big time,' I told him. Fear that something awful might have happened to Riko had taken over my brain. *I hate you, Bridget O'Reilly*, I thought. *This is all your fault.* But a nagging doubt at the back of my mind, told me that *she* wasn't to blame. *I* was.

'Jess, whatever's the matter?' asked a familiar voice.

I sat up, surprised to see that Aunt Maddie had just arrived. 'How did you get in?'

'I just bumped into your father. He let me through. But what's the matter, Jess? You look terrible.'

'Nothing's the matter.'

'Nothing? It doesn't look like nothing. Boy trouble?'

'No. *Pff*. Nothing like that.'

'Argument with Pia?'

I shook my head. My attempts to act normal weren't succeeding though because another wave of anxiety flooded through me. I felt I was going to burst if I didn't confide in someone. 'Oh, Aunt Maddie, I've done something *really* terrible.'

'It can't be that bad.'

'It *is*. Can I . . . can I trust you with the most *enormous* secret?'

Aunt Maddie came and put her arm around me. 'Of course you can, Jess. Now what is it?'

'Did Dad tell you about Riko going missing?'

She nodded. 'Poor Mr and Mrs Mori. They must be out of their minds with worry.'

'It's *my* fault.'

'Your fault? How could that be? Jess . . . Did you help her get away?'

'No. Nothing like that. *Worse*.'

'Worse?'

I nodded. 'Did you see that article about teens at Porchester Park?'

Aunt Maddie nodded. 'Your dad showed it to me.'

'I'm the reason Riko ran away. It was . . . it was *me* who blabbed to the press. *I'm* the . . . the anonymous source.'

Aunt Maddie's face registered shock. 'You? Oh, Jess, *no*—'

'*Yes*,' I sobbed. 'And you don't have to tell me how incredibly stupid it was. I know. I've been cursing myself all morning. Riko must have seen the article in the paper and run away and all because of me and my big mouth and . . . and . . . Dad will kill me if he ever finds out and he might lose his job and we'll have nowhere to live and Alisha will hate me and something might happen to Riko and you probably hate me too now and think I'm pathetic and so will Gran when she finds out and this is the worst day of my whole life apart from when Mum died and her funeral and I wish she was here but she'd probably hate me too and she'd be right because I totally hate myself.' I burst into tears.

Aunt Maddie let me cry for a few minutes then she made me a cup of sweet tea. I couldn't drink it. I couldn't swallow so Aunt Maddie sat next to me again and took my hand.

'Do you hate me?' I asked.

Aunt Maddie laughed softly. 'Oh no, Jess. I could never do that. And I'm glad you told me.'

'Well, if *you* don't hate me, I hate myself.'

'No. You mustn't do that. Part of growing up is learning about trust and who to open your heart to. Sadly some people who claim to be your friends aren't what they seem. It's one of life's harsh lessons, I'm afraid.'

'You can say that again.'

Aunt Maddie took a deep breath. 'You have to tell your dad, Jess. You *have* to. And the police. Any clue you have might help find her.'

'I can't. I'm scared. It won't make any difference.

Riko is still gone. I haven't a clue where she might be.'

'I know this must be frightening for you but you have to be brave. You made a mistake. Own up to it. That's part of growing up too. How you respond to situations is what makes you the person you are – and I know you to be a brave girl. There's no harm in making mistakes. Everyone makes them. The harm is in lying there cursing yourself and thinking you're a failure. Successful people make a mistake, own up to it then get up and say, I was wrong, how can I make it right? How can I make things better?'

I didn't like what I was hearing. Not one bit. I wanted to hide away and pretend none of it had happened. I didn't want to tell Dad or the police, but I knew that Aunt Maddie was right. I nodded. 'OK. Let's do it,' I said.

Aunt Maddie squeezed my hand then she called Dad on his mobile. He appeared at the house five minutes later, by which time I could hardly breathe.

'What's this all about?' asked Dad.

Aunt Maddie glanced at me. 'Jess has something she needs to say.'

Dad turned to look at me.

'I . . . I . . . Please don't be mad at me or at least, *be* mad at me, but I'm sorry, I truly am.'

Dad looked puzzled. 'What's this all about?' he repeated. 'Sorry for what?'

I took a deep breath. It was hard to even look at Dad but I made myself. 'It was me, Dad. I spoke to the press.'

Dad's face registered horror. '*You*, Jess? When?'

'Last week. I . . .'

Dad began to pace up and down and rub his head. 'Oh Christ . . .'

'I never thought she'd write about it. I mean, I never thought she'd want to write about *teenagers*. I thought they were off-limits. I thought she was outside waiting for a scoop about an A-lister. A big celeb. A grown-up. She was kind to me. I thought she was all right. I know, I'm such an idiot. Now I know you were right about not talking to them. I'm so sorry. I won't ever do it again.'

Dad stopped pacing and took a deep breath. 'You're telling me that the quotes came from you? *You're* the anonymous source?' It seemed like he couldn't take it in.

I nodded. 'Yes. *Yes*. Me. Are you mad with me? Stupid question. Of course you are.'

Dad sighed. He looked so worried. 'Not mad, Jess. Disappointed. Very disappointed,' he replied. Somehow, that felt even worse.

I began to apologise again but Dad didn't appear to be listening and stared out of the window as I burbled on. Finally he turned to Aunt Maddie and I. 'OK. Right. No-one needs to know who spoke to the press. None of this needs to go outside this room. Jess, I'm glad you told me so that I can stop the inquisition with my staff. It wasn't fair to let other people come under suspicion when you knew all along that you were to blame and we'll speak about that later. For now, though, I have to think straight about what's best to do. Oh dear … But you owning up won't change the situation and could do more damage than good for all of us because, quite honestly, my reputation will be in ruins, not to mention how the residents would view you.'

'That's what I thought,' I blurted. 'That's why I didn't tell you.'

'She *is* sorry, Michael,' said Aunt Maddie. 'No-one could be angrier with her than she is with herself. I think she's learnt her lesson.'

'Never mind that. Riko is still missing and that's what's important. Being sorry doesn't let you off the hook, Jess,' said Dad in a cold voice. 'However, I have the apartment block to think about and if it got out that my daughter, *my* daughter, was the leak, it would reflect very badly. For now though, we have to do what we can to remedy the situation. You have to tell me anything you know so I can pass it on to the police.'

I nodded. 'I'll do anything I can to help but I have no idea where Riko might have gone. We weren't close.'

'But you *did* spend some time with her. She must have said *something*. Any detail might help.'

I searched my mind for anything I might have overlooked. I replayed our conversations in my head. 'I always felt there was *something* going on with her,' I said.

'Like what?' asked Aunt Maddie with a glance at Dad. 'Explain. How?'

'Like . . . I felt she was using me and Pia. She kept saying she wanted to be friends but it never felt real, not like with Alisha. It was like she was using us to get out on her own for a short time – away from her dad and her minder. That's all she wanted, a bit of freedom.

'Oh! But there's something else!' I exclaimed as I

remembered the nagging feeling I always had that Riko had a secret. 'It might be nothing.'

'What, Jess?' Dad urged.

'A boy. I thought I'd seen a boy hanging around. That why I went to talk to Bridget in the first place – to ask if she'd seen him too. He was there before Christmas and at first, I thought he was one of the paparazzi but he looked too young and not all pally with them like they are with each other. Then I thought he might be a tourist, you know, just having a nose. But the first time I went out with Riko to Harrods, she disappeared for a while when she went to the Ladies. Pia and I were well freaked.'

'And was the boy there, then?'

'I'm not sure. Riko reappeared but, before that, when I went looking for her, I thought I saw her with someone on the escalator but I couldn't be sure. I couldn't see him properly and I wasn't even certain it was her actually *with* someone or if he was just standing next to her on the escalator. It was so crowded and I was well freaked out myself.'

'Why didn't you mention this when you came back? You knew Mr Mori had trusted you to stay with her,' said Dad.

'Well, that's just it. I was mad with her for

disappearing, so was Pia, but she begged us not to say anything about her going off and she turned up again so it seemed there was no harm done. She said her dad wouldn't ever let her out again if he thought she'd lost us. I didn't know whether to believe her but she hadn't actually done anything wrong.'

'And this boy, have you seen him since?' Dad asked.

I shook my head. 'When we went to the cinema, Riko acted weird again, like she was looking for someone before we went in and then when we took our seats, she kept texting someone. I thought I saw the boy outside the cinema but after that, Riko was with me the whole time. I began to think I was being over-paranoid but just in case, I asked Bridget if she'd seen anyone hanging about outside here.'

'And had she?' asked Aunt Maddie.

'She said she'd seen a boy a few times but not really taken much notice. People are always staring at Porchester Park. Do you think he might be a stalker?'

Dad stood up. 'He could be anyone. He could be someone she knows or someone she's met on the Internet. Some girls can be very gullible. I'm going to call the police right now and tell them what you've told me. Whoever he is, you've given a very valuable clue, Jess. I have to pass it on immediately. In the meantime, we have to pray that she's not in any danger.'

Dad went to make his call and within ten minutes, he came back with a young police officer who'd been questioning staff who worked at the apartments. He held out a photograph to me. I glanced down at it.

'You father says you've seen someone hanging about a few times,' said the officer. 'Do you recognise the boy in this photo?'

It was the boy I'd seen outside Porchester Park. I nodded. 'That's him,' I said.

The officer took the photo back.

'Do you know who he is?' I asked.

'I'm afraid I can't divulge that information at this stage of the investigation. More to the point though, do *you* know who he is?

'No.'

'Is there anything else you can remember apart from what your father has already told us?'

'No.'

The police officer stared at me. 'Hmm.'

I felt a rising panic and once again, found it hard to breathe. I was sure he could see right into me, that he knew I was the one who had caused this whole sorry mess, but then he looked away and I felt the iron grip in my stomach relax a little.

'Thank you, Jess. You've been very helpful. Thank you very much. Well done.' He left, already talking into his mobile as he went.

Well done, he'd said. If only he knew the truth!

13
Search party

Everyone was round the table. Meg, Flo, Charlie, Henry and Tom, even Pia had raced back from her shopping trip.

'What can we do to help?' asked Tom.

After the police had gone, I'd sent out an alert to all my mates. I had a plan. The police were doing what they could. In the meantime, I'd decided to organise a search party of my own.

'Henry. You and Pia take Harrods,' I said.

'Isn't it getting a bit late now?' asked Meg.

'Never too late,' I said. I had actually thought the same thing myself but I had to do *something*.

Pia saluted me and grinned at Henry. 'Yessir.'

'Flo and Meg, you do Westfield. Riko said her idea of heaven would be to explore a mall without a minder and Westfield is the closest and biggest.'

'But we don't now what she looks like,' said Flo. "Better I go with Charlie. He'd recognise her.' She gave Charlie a coy look which was lost on him.

And it would give you a chance to spend time with my brother, I thought. *Smart girl*. She'd obviously read the last facebook update and seen the message about sharing a mutual project with a boy.

'Good plan,' I said. 'OK with you, Chaz?'

Charlie nodded. 'Maybe I'd better take Meg too. Westfield is a big place. And Tom, probably best you go with Jess because she knows what she looks like.' I had to stifle a giggle. It seemed everyone had been reading the facebook updates. I just hoped that Tom hadn't wised up.

Tom smiled and gave me a look that made my toes curl. I felt conflicted. Part of me was still in deep shame about blabbing to Bridget but another part of me was doing cartwheels, thinking, *Wahey. Time alone with the love god*. People are complicated. *I'm* complicated. So many emotions and all in the space of sixty seconds!

*

'So, where to?' asked Tom when we got outside and the others had gone off on their various missions through the snow which had started to fall mid afternoon.

Back to your house for a snog session, I thought. God, if my thoughts came out of my mouth, I'd be in deep trouble. *Focus, Jess*.

'Good question. She could be anywhere. Um—'

'We have to start somewhere,' he interrupted. 'Have the police let on who the boy might be?'

I shook my head. 'They weren't giving anything away. She might know him but he might also be a stalker or, worst case scenario, someone she met on the Internet who's lured her away.'

'Well, we have to hope it's not that,' said Tom. 'I bet he's her boyfriend. That's what I reckon after what you've told us so far. She probably just wants some time alone with him.'

'You think? But where would they go?'

Tom shrugged. 'Depends on who he is and whether his parents live in London.'

'I guess the police will have all that covered.'

'So let's think,' he said and looked deeply into my eyes. 'Where would *you* go if you had some time with someone you really fancied and it was your first opportunity to hang out with them?'

I felt myself blush. *He has read the facebook update*, I thought.

Behind us, I noticed Eddie, the homeless man in his usual pitch in the doorway. I nodded at him and he looked away. He was there most days now. No matter how many times he was moved on, he always came back. Suddenly I had an idea and went over to him.

'Hey, Eddie, you didn't happen to notice a Japanese girl leaving the apartment block over there this morning, did you? Maybe with a boy?'

'I see lots,' he said. 'Many boys, many girls, many people.'

I pointed over at Porchester Park. 'A girl who lives over there. You saw her with me one morning. A Japanese girl. Very striking. Mad clothes.'

Eddie nodded. 'I did see her. Very early. She got into a taxi.'

'With a boy?'

He nodded.

'You didn't happen to hear where they were going, did you?'

Eddie stayed silent. Tom fished around for some coins and handed him a pound. Eddie looked at it then back up. I looked in my purse and added another.

'It's all we've got, Eddie, apart from loose change and we might need that if we're going to look for her. She's gone missing. Please. Her parents are out of their mind with worry.'

Eddie took the second coin. 'St Pancras,' he said. 'I heard the boy say St Pancras. They'll be halfway across Europe by now.'

'Halfway across Europe?' I asked.

Tom nodded. 'Eurostar,' he said. 'The Eurostar goes from there.'

I had a sudden flash. Riko's perfect holiday. 'Does it go to Paris?'

'Yup,' said Tom. 'Why?'

'I bet that's where she's going. Come on.'

I took his hand and pulled him towards the tube station.

'Why would she go there?' Tom asked as we skidded along the pavement. The snow was already beginning to turn to slush. I filled him in on my conversation with Riko and her perfect day being in Paris with a boy she liked. ' . . . See? That has to be it.'

Tom stopped. 'Don't you think we ought to tell the police? It's a valuable clue.'

'I guess,' I said. 'I don't have a number for them but I'll call Dad.'

Tom glanced at his watch. 'Jess, it's almost three o'clock. Surely she'll have gone by now.'

I felt a sinking feeling hit my stomach. He was probably right but I couldn't give up and just sit and wait for news. I had to at least go and look. 'Please Tom. I have to try.'

Tom nodded. 'Sure. Let's go.'

I dialled Dad's mobile but it went to voicemail. 'Dad, it's Jess. We think Riko might have gone to St Pancras to catch the Eurostar to Paris. She told me that would be her perfect day out. You'd better let the police know. I . . . I'm going to the station now.'

'Got your Oyster card?' asked Tom as he got his out. 'Or do we need to get a ticket?'

I pulled out my card and waved it at him. 'If the police get there, she might freak and run. Can you imagine? I think our best chance is to get there, find her, and persuade her to come back. Less trouble all around.'

Tom looked doubtful but didn't argue. He got out his iPhone and started pressing the keys.

'What are you looking for?' I asked.

'Train times to Paris.' He glanced up a few minutes later. 'Bummer. They go almost *every* half hour.'

'Half hour? Oh *no*.'

'Either they've been planning this and booked a particular journey or they're chancing it but they'll have been lucky to just walk onto a train. I think it gets booked up months ahead.'

'Maybe they didn't know that,' I said. 'I didn't and Riko's not exactly familiar with public transport. We've nothing to lose, have we? Let's still go, if only because someone there might have seen her. She does stand out with her unique style.'

We flew down into the tube, through the turnstiles and onto the escalator. A man was blocking the way on the left-hand-side.

'Excuse me,' said Tom. The man gave him a filthy look and stayed put.

'Er, excuse me, sir, but the left-hand-side of the escalator is for people in a rush. The right-hand-side is for people who wish to stand still,' Tom said politely.

The man moved aside but looked very disgruntled.

'Thank you,' I said as we hurried past.

At the bottom of the escalator a group of Italian tourists were gathered, blocking the way of anyone trying to get off. I almost tripped over Tom but luckily one of them saw us and moved the others out of the way just in time. We hurtled on to the right platform where the display said that there was a train in five minutes.

'Phew,' I said. 'It's straight through to King's Cross, then St Pancras is just over the road.'

At that moment, the notice board showed a change in information. *CORRECTION. CORRECTION*, it flashed in big yellow letters. Then a message came up that the next train would be in fifteen minutes.

'*Fifteen* minutes. Oh *no!*' I gasped.

'We just have to chill, Jess. We'll get there and hopefully your dad will have got your message by now and Mission Rescue Riko will be sorted,' said Tom.

I glanced around. 'I guess. Still it's not like in the movies is it? If we were in a movie, we'd be in and out of fast cars—'

'Then a helicopter—'

'And a speedboat that turns into a submarine then a plane.'

'And finally we'd parachute down onto the platform at St Pancras.'

Tom did a karate move then pointed back at himself. 'Agent 007. Licensed to thrill.'

I watched the tube platform fill up with irate

travellers who seemed as unhappy about the delay as we were. 'Instead we're stuck in the underground with hundreds of others,' I said. 'Maybe they're all on secret rescue missions too.'

Finally the train arrived and we got on. We stood in the aisle so others could sit down. As the tube rattled off, there was a lurch and I lost my footing and fell into Tom. He steadied me then put his arm around me. 'Agent Hall,' he said. 'You really must stop drinking when on an assignment.'

'Sorry, Agent Robertson,' I said. 'I will join AA and deal with my problem as soon as our mission is completed. Hic!'

We spent the rest of the journey with his arm around me to steady me and instead of feeling in a rush, I now felt that I'd like the journey to go on forever but all too soon, we were at King's Cross. We got off and raced up to ground level, taking the final steps two at a time. We darted across the street, dodging taxis and cars and into St Pancras station. It was heaving with people, all seemingly in a hurry, pulling cases, looking for platforms, watching departures. Even the cafés looked crowded, with travellers at every table and in queues at the counters.

'Ohmigod, this is worse than Harrods!' I exclaimed. 'We'll never find her. It's hopeless.' Riko had disappeared early morning and it was now well into rush hour and the station was swarming with travellers rushing to get home. 'It's too late.'

'Hey, Hall. Where's your fighting spirit? It's not over yet,' said Tom. 'If this *was* a movie, we wouldn't be giving up, would we?'

I shook my head but inside, I felt desperate. I knew that it wasn't a movie. This was real. Someone had gone missing and I'd had a part to play in that.

'Let's go to the Eurostar departure area,' said Tom. 'In the meantime, call your dad and check he got the message.'

I got my phone out and started to call Dad when it bleeped that the battery was low. 'Nooooooooo. My phone! It's dead. I . . . I meant to recharge it, but . . .'

Tom handed me his. 'Use mine.'

'I don't know how to use one of those,' I said. I felt stupid. He'd think I was so uncool. I'd make a crap secret agent.

'Give me the number and I'll call,' he said as he took it back.

'07856 ... no. 08956 ... Oh NO! I can't remember his number. I never use it. It's on automatic dial on my phone. I ...'

I felt even more stupid than ever now. Tom laughed and pretended to talk into his phone. 'Agent Q. Agent Hall hasn't recharged her phone. Recommend you send her to rehab in Botswana for a few years to recharge her brain.'

'Dad might be trying to get hold of me after the message I left earlier,' I said. 'Oh God, my life is over. He'll kill me when he finds he can't get through to me. He's always on at me to leave my phone on and keep it recharged.'

'Chill, Agent Hall. It happens to everyone.'

Just at that moment, I spotted Riko in the distance. She was with the boy from the photo and they were looking in a shop window. They were chatting away like friends which was a huge relief. She wouldn't have been that relaxed if she was being kidnapped. I pulled on Tom's arm. 'She's there! I saw her. Going into that shoe shop now and she's with him. Come on.'

We ran along the arcade and up to the shop, where we skidded to a halt and hid round the corner. I tiptoed out and peeked through the window and indeed, there she was, trying on shoes like she didn't have a care in the world. Tom came up behind me but I pulled him back before she saw us. 'I can't believe she's trying on shoes when the police are out looking for her!'

'Why not?' He glanced at his watch. 'She doesn't know they're looking for her. Maybe they've got a ticket and are just killing time, like the rest of them.' He indicated the station with all its shops and cafés. 'And let's face it, this is as good a place to hang out as anywhere.'

'We have to let someone know that she's here. What time's the next train?'

Tom looked at the board. 'Twenty minutes then another in fifty.'

I peeked around the corner and into the window again to check she was still there. Whoops! I looked straight into Riko's eyes. I don't know which of us looked more shocked. She turned around and said something to the boy with her, who turned and glared at me.

'Damn. They've seen me,' I said. 'What do we do now?'

'We confront her,' said Tom and he pulled me out into the open but it was too late. We saw the back of

Riko and the boy as they hurried out of the shop and off into the crowd.

'First we have to let someone know,' said Tom. 'I'll call Charlie. I should have thought of it before. I'm a crap agent too. God, it's not as easy as it looks being James Bond. Charlie can call your dad and Pia and she can call her mum.'

We stopped for a moment while he made the calls and luckily, got through to both of them.

'The cavalry are coming,' he said when he'd finished. 'They're all on their way. Now, let's try and find Riko before she gets on a train!'

'No point. It will take the others forty minutes or so to get here. She'll be long gone by then.'

'Depends which train she's on,' said Tom. 'And that's if they've managed to get on one. Never give up until it's over, Hall. In the meantime, let's try and find her.' He gave me a quick hug and pulled me in the direction Riko had gone.

The next fifteen minutes really was like something from a movie as we gave chase to Riko and the boy. We spotted her on an escalator going up. We hopped on, only to see her get on an escalator going down a few moments later. She even waved. She was clearly enjoying herself. We followed them in and out of shops but they always seemed to be one step ahead of us. At one point, they disappeared around a corner then reappeared on the other side of the arcade. Riko saw us and grinned like she was having the time of her life.

'I will *kill* her. This is getting ridiculous. A waste of time,' I panted after we'd been in and out of a newsagent's, a book shop and a clothes store.

'I don't think so,' said Tom. 'At least we've established one thing and that is that the boy with her is definitely *not* a kidnapper or a stalker. She clearly knows him and is comfortable with him.'

'Her boyfriend . . .'

Tom's phone rang. He took the call as we raced on to the next shop where a glimpse of a pink coat alerted us to Riko's presence. 'Charlie says he's just spoken to your dad and the police will be here any minute.'

'Quick, Tom. I don't think she's seen us. She went into the chemist.'

We ran after her, past the cosmetics, round a corner then *WHAM*. Face to face with Riko and the boy.

'Jess! Oh!' She turned and started to run with the boy.

'No! Riko. Don't,' I called after her. 'Please stop.'

She stopped and turned back. Her whole body looked stiff with anger. '*What* do you want? *What* are you doing here?'

'We've been trying to find *you*. Don't you realise what you've done? Your parents are freaking out. They have the police looking for you.'

Riko looked around her. '*Police*? Shit. Ashton, what shall we do?'

The boy went pale. He shrugged his shoulders as if to say that he had no idea.

'Are you going to Paris?' I asked.

Riko shook her head. 'Yes. No. All the trains are booked.'

Tom gave me a look as if to say, I told you so.

'So you're going home?' I asked.

'No way,' she said. 'We're waiting for a cancellation.'

'Riko, you don't get it do you?' I said. 'Your parents are well worried about you. They haven't a clue where you are or what's happened.'

'Chill. I was going to call my parents. I was only going to go for a couple of days. It would have been fine if *you* hadn't interfered.'

'What planet are you on, Riko?' I asked. 'You must have known they'd miss you.'

Riko stared at me angrily. 'I just wanted some time alone with Ashton. They treat me like a kid. I just want some time out! Can you blame me?'

'No. Well, yes actually. You're in big trouble and it wasn't because of me interfering. They knew you'd gone straight away. Listen, let me call Dad and say we're all coming back.'

'Nooooo,' Riko cried.

She looked at the boy, who shrugged. 'I don't know, Riko, The police are involved. I . . . I guess we ought to go back.' He sounded American.

Riko rolled her eyes. 'You total cop-out. This was to be our holiday, Ash. *Ours*. We've been planning it for weeks.'

The boy looked sheepish. Up close, he had a gentle air about him and I got the feeling that the whole venture was Riko's idea.

'If we go now, we can avoid a big scene when the police arrive,' I suggested.

'I don't care. I want to get arrested,' said Riko. 'That'll teach my dad.'

'He cares about you, Riko. I saw how upset he was. Come on, see sense. The operation must have cost the police thousands. They aren't going to see it as a joke and you might get into trouble.'

Riko folded her arms as if shutting out the world. 'You have no sense of adventure, Jess.'

Tom stepped forward. 'She does, actually, but this is no time for fun. Come on. We're going back. If we get the Piccadilly line, we can maybe avert the police and be back at Porchester Park in about forty minutes.'

Riko wrinkled her nose. 'The *tube*? You must be joking. I'm Riko Mori. I don't do tubes.'

Tom stood very close to her face. 'Listen, Riko Mori. I don't care whether you do or don't do tubes but you are going *home*. Understand?'

Riko tried to stand up to him but he eyeballed her right back. In the end, her posture slumped slightly. 'OK. I'm bored with this game anyway. It so isn't turning out the way I planned. We'll come . . . but we'll get a taxi. Right?'

Tom glanced at me. 'OK. But you pay, right?'

'Why? Can't afford it?' sneered Riko.

'You're the problem. The problem pays,' said Tom firmly.

I glanced over at him. It was amazing the way he'd taken control of the situation and kept me going when I was ready to give up. *My hero*, I thought.

'I . . . I might make my own way back,' said Ashton. 'The police are looking for you, Riko, yeah? Best I don't get involved.'

Riko's face registered a flicker of hurt which she quickly covered up. 'Sure. Desert us now, why don't you?'

Ashton looked at the ground again and shifted on his feet. 'Come on Riko. You know I could get expelled for this, not to mention what my folks are going to say. At least they knew I was out for the day. I'm sorry, I can't get blamed for this.'

Riko flung her arms out. 'OK. Go. I didn't really want to go with you anyway.'

Ashton sighed. 'I'll call you,' he said as he backed away.

'Don't bother,' said Riko. She stuck her bottom lip out and looked like a five-year-old who was going to cry. For a brief second, I felt sorry for her as Ashton disappeared into the crowds. Rich or poor, boy problems were still the same.

We made our way to the taxi queue and, as we waited, Tom called Charlie to tell him to let Dad know that we were on our way back. Then he called

Pia and told her to get the others to meet us back at Porchester Park.

Just as we got into the taxi and were driving away, I noticed police vans with their sirens screeching, advancing towards the station.

'Bet they're coming for you,' I said.

'Oops, missed us,' she said sarcastically. 'Come to get little old me, too late, guys, too late. But hey, Jess . . . One favour. Even though he's a stinking cowardly rat and I hate him, please don't bring Ashton into this. When we get back, say you found me but that I was on my own.'

'But the police already have a photo of him.'

'Yes but only *you* know that he was actually with me. They have no proof. Please. He was right. He might get expelled and his parents can be as intense as mine. I don't care if I get into trouble but . . . I don't want him to as well.'

I glanced at Tom. 'What do you think?'

He thought for a moment then nodded. 'Fine,' he said. 'No need to bring him into it unless they look on the cameras at St Pancras. Don't forget they're everywhere.'

'But if I'm back home, safe and sorry etc, they probably won't check the cameras. I'd say it would be a waste of police time and money,' said Riko, but she didn't sound that confident. She stared out of the window for a few minutes. 'I would have gone back,' she said finally. 'We would have got a return ticket. I just wanted a bit of time out.'

'That's what the paper said,' said Tom.

'What paper?' asked Riko.

'The article. I . . . Oh. I thought you'd seen it. I . . . I thought that's why you took off,' I said.

'What are you talking about?' asked Riko. 'What article?'

My mind was putting together the pieces. So she hadn't read the article and freaked? Of course not. She said she'd been planning her escape all along. 'Um. It doesn't matter. Nothing. Not important. You didn't see it. So . . . do you mean you were going to go off with Ashton anyway?'

Riko nodded. 'We'd been planning to go somewhere for weeks – a few days out, anywhere. It was when you asked what my perfect holiday was, remember, Jess?'

I nodded. 'A day in Paris.'

'Yeah, said Riko. 'That gave me the idea. I thought why not? A day trip to Paris. Our plan was to go, call my parents when we got there, when no-one could reach us and be back the following evening. At least that was the plan. Neither of us thought to book ahead. We always have someone who takes care of that sort of thing. I just assumed you pitched up, got your ticket and off you went. We were told that there might be a place if someone cancelled or didn't show – that's what we were waiting for when you turned up and ruined everything.'

'We didn't ruin anything,' said Tom. 'If anything, we saved your bacon.'

'Whatever,' said Riko. 'But, rewind a sec. *Paper*? What are you talking about?'

'One of the journalists who hangs about outside where you live did an article. Teens at the top, that sort of the thing,' Tom explained.

'So what did it say?' she said and preened herself. 'Did it mention me?'

I felt a sinking feeling in my stomach. Tom didn't know I was the anonymous source.

'It did actually,' Tom continued. 'It was about how a lot of so-called privileged teens like you find it hard finding friends and get lonely.'

Riko scowled. 'I've got friends. I've got friends at school. So was it saying I was a *loser?*'

'No,' I said. 'Just that it can be lonely sometimes.'

Riko's expression grew harder. She tapped on the

glass partition. 'Hey, driver. Stop at a newsagent. I want to get a paper.'

'And who are you, the Queen?' said the driver. I could see in the mirror that he rolled his eyes. 'Kids these days, no bloody manners.' All the same, he slowed down and stopped at the next newsagent. Riko got out swiftly, followed by Tom.

'You stay here, Jess. I'm not going to risk her running off,' he said.

'Whatever,' snarled Riko.

They reappeared a few minutes later and Riko stood on the pavement. I watched as she read the article. When she'd finished, she climbed back into the taxi with Tom. She had a face like thunder.

'It's you, isn't it?' she demanded. 'The anonymous source?'

'Hey, give Jess a break,' said Tom. 'You can't lay everything on her. If anything, you should be thanking her.'

'So much you know,' said Riko, turning back to the paper as the taxi drove off again.

I didn't know what to do. I didn't want Tom to think I was a traitor.

Riko threw the paper aside. 'This will *kill* my street cred,' she said. 'I sound like a sad, pathetic loser.'

'Tomorrow's fish-and-chip paper—' I started.

Riko turned on me. 'What are you on about now? It's *you* who's the sad loser, Jess Hall. I know it was you, even if you aren't admitting it. This is almost word for word what I said to you.'

'I *said*, lay off Jess, Riko,' said Tom. He took my hand and held it.

Riko folded her arms and gave me the filthiest look.

I felt awful. I'd agreed with Dad that we wouldn't reveal it was me who was the source so I wasn't going to go against his orders again. As the taxi headed towards Knightsbridge, I felt my eyes fill with tears, tears that Riko noticed. She narrowed her eyes but there was no sympathy there, only hatred.

14
New year, new possibilities

Gran was back from Italy and we were all round her house for a belated celebration. Her house smelt festive from the roast dinner cooking in the kitchen and from the apple-and-cinnamon drinks she'd prepared for us when we arrived. Us being Dad, Aunt Maddie, Pia, Charlie, Mrs Carlsen and me. Even though it was January the fourth, me and Charlie were wearing our Christmas jumpers, plus I'd made a tinsel tiara to complete the look. It was tradition to look like an eejit and always would be. I breathed in the familiar, safe scent of Gran's and sighed deeply. She was back. All was well in my world again.

'Ah . . . Christmas,' I said.

'Only it's January,' Charlie pointed out.

'Christmas is a feeling,' I said, 'not a specific date and that's what I'm going to write my essay about for school.'

'I'd go along with that,' said Charlie and he broke into song. 'Oh, I wish it could be Christmas every da-a-ay.'

Pia and I joined in by doing our version of street dancing which made Charlie stop singing. 'Mad,' he said as he shook his head. 'Sad.'

Gran had had the most brilliant time in Florence and done some fantastic drawings of nudie people. She was already planning an exhibition up in Hampstead at a gallery who liked her work. She shooed us out of the kitchen so that she could concentrate on preparing the meal, so Pia and I headed upstairs with Aunt Maddie. It was makeover time.

Pia covered the mirror in Gran's bedroom with a shawl so that Aunt Maddie couldn't see herself, then she grimaced and pulled faces as we plucked her eyebrows. Once they'd been shaped into a lovely arch, Pia applied a little light make-up then I blow-dried her hair. Once that was done, we pulled out a selection of clothes for Aunt Maddie to try on. I'd brought them from home and they were from Mum's wardrobe. I couldn't give them away to anyone after she'd died so I'd kept them in boxes. However, I knew she'd have liked to know that they'd gone to Aunt Maddie. Mum was always bullying people to wear their good clothes every day and not save them for special occasions. She would have hated to think that her best were wasting away in storage.

First Aunt Maddie tried a black wrap dress. It looked great on her and made her look loads slimmer than the baggy fleeces she usually wore. Next was a green skirt cut on the bias with a coral cardi and a little camisole top. That looked good too. As we pulled out more and more clothes, they all looked a million times better than Aunt Maddie's old wardrobe. In the end, we settled for the cardi and skirt.

'Ta-dah,' said Pia as she finally whipped the shawl away from the mirror.

Aunt Maddie's eyes filled with tears as she looked at her reflection. 'I look like Eleanor,' she said.

I nodded. The likeness had always been there but Mum had always been the more stylish one. I felt my eyes fill with tears too. She wasn't my mum and never would be but she was Mum's sister. She was family. While Mum was alive, I'd never appreciated having an aunt. She was just someone who came to visit occasionally and who often, used to annoy me, but lately I'd felt closer to Aunt Maddie. I'd begun to appreciate that, in her own way, she was there for me.

'Watch out world,' I said and went and gave her a hug.

'Come and sit at the table,' called Gran from downstairs.

Dinner was soon served with all the trimmings and as we sat around the table, I thought what a strange Christmas it had been: up, down and round and round, feeling good, feeling bad, spending time with the rich, with the poor, on an adventure with Tom. I would make a note of that in my essay too – that Christmas could be many things to many people and it wasn't always a happy time. Sometimes it could be mixed, like it had been for me. I hadn't heard from Tom since the Rescue Riko mission. I was *so* disappointed because I'd felt close to him that day and we'd had a good time together. Made a good team. Since then though, he'd only been in touch to speak to Charlie about music and I was beginning to think that he just wasn't into having a relationship. He might like to hang out with me when it suited him but nothing more. I was still nobody's girl.

As Gran passed around the roasties and the cranberry sauce, I picked up the stuffing.

'This makes me think of Tom,' I said. 'He can go stuff himself.'

Pia almost choked on a sprout.

Later that evening, Alisha skyped me from the holiday home where she was staying.

'We saw the article about Porchester Park,' she said. 'Dad gets the English papers while we're away.'

God! Straight to the point, I thought. I'd been hoping to skirt around the subject for a while then maybe drop it into the conversation to test if she'd seen it. I wondered if, like Riko, she'd guessed that it was me who had leaked the story. I had to make a decision. I thought about my resolution not to trust so easily. Could I trust Alisha? She was my mate, and mates trust each other, so I decided that she deserved to know the truth.

'Alisha, I have something to tell you and I hope you won't hate me—' I started.

'You're the anonymous source.'

'Oh! How did you know?'

'Put two and two together.'

'I'm *so* sorry. I didn't mean to—'

Alisha nodded. 'Tell me everything,' she said. Her face over the camera didn't give anything away and I felt my palms sweat as I quickly filled her in on the whole Riko escapade.

'Hmm,' she said finally. 'Bummer.'

'I've been dreading you finding out in case you don't want to be friends any more and I wouldn't blame you.'

Alisha shrugged. 'Hey Jess, we all make mistakes, believe me, I've been there. When Dad first started to be newsworthy, all sorts of people wanted to be my friends. People who'd never given me the time of day at school before. Suddenly I was Miss Popular. It's true what the article said. You don't know who to trust or what people's motives are. I blabbed my mouth off to someone in the press and next day it was all over the papers. Dad was so cool about it. He just said, lesson learnt, end of story. I'll say the same thing to you. Lesson learnt?'

'Lesson learnt. Does the rest of your family know it was me?'

Alisha shook her head, then grinned. 'Nah. They're not as smart as me.'

'I'll never trust a journalist again,' I said.

'Actually, no,' said Alisha. 'You have to be wary but some of them are OK. They're just people doing their job. Some are snakes, no doubt about it, and they'll do anything to get a story then twist it to get a good headline but some of them are good writers and will do a good piece. You've got to distinguish between the two. I had to learn that too.'

'Maybe, but I never want to go through that again.'

'Poor Jess. I can imagine.'

'So, still mates?'

'Still mates,' she said. 'What happened to Riko?'

'Sent back to school double-quick. It was meant to be a punishment but actually, she'd have been happy about it. She was missing her mates.'

'As the article said.'

'She doesn't exactly know it was me who blabbed because I didn't admit it to her but like you, she guessed. Please don't tell anyone. No-one else knows apart from you, Pia, Aunt Maddie and Dad.'

'Your secret's safe with me, Jess, and I'm glad you feel you can trust me enough to tell the truth.'

'That's what mates do, even if it's harsh.'

Alisha looked well chuffed. 'Yeah. So, how's your Christmas been?'

'Mixed. Story of my life. I go from joy to despair and all in the space of five minutes.'

Alisha laughed. 'Welcome to my world. My mum says it's our hormones. Whatever, it makes us interesting. How's the boy research?'

'I've closed the page down. I'm going to leave it as one of life's great unsolved mysteries. I've realised they really are an alien species. I have no idea what goes on in their heads.'

'Me neither,' said Alisha with a laugh. 'Hey, just a sec. JJ's just come in. He wants to say hi.'

JJ appeared beside her on my screen.

'Hey there, Miss UK,' he said and flashed his killer smile.

'Hey yourself. How's things?'

'Great. We got some good skiing in. It's been great. Quiet but chilled, you know?'

'And is your girlfriend still with you?'

JJ shook his head. 'She went back to the States.'

Alisha nudged him aside and her face filled the screen again. 'Big lesson for my bro this Christmas and that is, you can't ever go back. Got to move on, hey JJ?'

'Butt out,' he said and pushed her out of the way. 'I'm talking to Jess. As I was saying, Jess, yes, I have learnt to move on, which is why I'm looking forward to coming back and picking up where *we* left off.'

Alisha nudged him out of the way again. 'Woo-oo. Flirt alert. Is something going on here that I don't know about?'

'None of your business,' said JJ.

'Jess?' asked Alisha.

'I . . . nn . . .'

Alisha grinned. 'I get it, Miss UK. Just don't go breaking his heart.'

'As if,' I said. So Tom wasn't interested, but maybe JJ was. Suddenly my future had just got a whole lot brighter.

After they'd gone, I took a hamper of food from Gran's out for Eddie. He was curled up in a blanket, asleep in his usual doorway.

'Happy New Year, Eddie,' I said quietly, as I put the box down next to him so that he'd find it when he woke up 'I wish I could do more.'

To his far left, I noticed there were a couple of paparazzi hanging about. No sign of Bridget. She hadn't been seen in days. She'd got her story and moved on, leaving me with a dull ache when I thought of her, but a lesson well and truly learned, and that is that not everyone who befriends you is your friend.

As I made my way back to Porchester Park, I remembered that Dad had asked me to drop an envelope into an apartment on the first floor. I went back inside, collected it from his office, made my way across the reception to the lift where I pressed the button for the first floor. The lift appeared seconds later and the doors opened.

'Just a sec,' said a voice behind me. I turned to see the most divine apparition had pressed the hold button. I felt as if my heart had stopped, as well as the lift. This boy wasn't handsome. He wasn't cute. He was one hundred percent *beautiful.* Tall and blond with an amazing jawline, high cheekbones and piercing blue eyes.

'Hi, I'm Alexei,' he said in the sexiest of foreign accents. 'You must be Jess.'

'Umf,' I said.

'I was hoping to bump into you,' the boy continued. 'My father told me that Mr Hall had a daughter and a son. I've been away at school many years but now I am to go to classes here. I don't know many people so I hope we can become friends. Forgive me being forward, but, how else I make friends?'

I gave him my best smile. 'Yeah sure,' I said, trying to sound casual. Inside, I felt like I'd had a shot of adrenaline and could do cartwheels across the hall. *Ding dong merrily on high, in heaven the bells are ringing*, I thought as I got out a scrap of paper and wrote my phone number and email address on it for him.

A new year, a new chapter, new possibilities!

www.milliondollarmatesbooks.co.uk